The Old Eve Tree

JS Fairchild

Love is Love...
Judy

Praise for *The Old Eve Tree*

Terry H.
An unforgettable story filled with life lessons and love, teaching us all how to be better humans and how to love unconditionally.

Lisa C.
I have absolutely been so engrossed in this story! Such a good thing to write about and so sad how people had to live in fear back then.

Hannah
The whole story has a "To Kill a Mockingbird" feel with how the story draws out your own feelings on injustice and standing up for what's right.

Dolores W.
I couldn't stop reading. I love Tilly and her "family" of interesting characters.

Linda L.
The book embodies so many emotions and rich images, and it challenges fundamental beliefs.

Stacy M.
Great suspense! I kept being surprised! This book is so full of love, even through the awful parts. I felt the love surrounding and binding the story.

The Old Eve Tree

JS Fairchild

The Old Eve Tree
By JS Fairchild

For more information, please see *About the Author* at the close of this book.

Cover photo by Dmytro Kosmenko/istockphoto.

Cover and interior design, formatting, and production art by Donna Marie Benjamin.

Ordering information: Quantity sales. Special discounts are available on quantity purchases by book clubs, corporations, associations, and others. For details, contact the publisher at the address above.

ISBN 978-0-932624-11-6

1. Main category— [Fiction General] 2. Other categories— [Fiction Historical General]

© 2022
Elevation Press
Cedaredge, Colorado
www.elevation-press-books.com

Acknowledgments

I owe a debt of gratitude to Sherry White for the hours she spent reading and rereading this manuscript and offering her invaluable suggestions. She is a smart and giving friend! I also wish to express my gratitude to Don and Donna Marie Benjamin and Elevation Press for helping me give birth to this book. And I want Mark to know he is my Grandpa Poe.

On Friday morning, the day after Thanksgiving 2016, this entire story flashed through my mind at 3:37 in the morning. The narrative took time to create, but the story never left its mark. I hope you enjoy the read!

—JS Fairchild/June 16, 2022

Arkansas, 1952

Chapter 1

I was sicker than a damn dog, and I mean it! In all my seven years, nobody told me I shouldn't save my most beautiful Easter egg, then eat it a month later. It sure enough looked fine to me. So, when I headed out a the house yesterday to go fishin' at the back creek, I took it with me. I packed some other stuff too, just in case I needed a little fortification when I got there, but I was real anxious to chomp into that egg.

The night 'fore Easter last month, Momma2 boiled a bunch of eggs our hens laid and set out colored water fer Junie Bird and me. We fought 'bout the colors. We was always fightin' over who got what. Junie Bird had a habit of pickin' out her favorite of whatever we had comin' to us and settin' her sights on gettin' it first. She wanted the red color, and that was *my* favorite. I pitched a fit about it, and Momma2 ended up takin' it away 'til we used up all the other colors. I thought I'd die waitin' for that red color. Junie Bird is so damn slow at everything she does. By the time she finished usin' the other colors, I thought the eggs would hatch. When Junie Bird finally finished, Momma2 handed me the red water. She let me go first 'cuz I was the youngest. Junie Bird sat and pouted, and I let her. She wasn't gonna bother me while I got a chance to get at that red colorin'. That's when I made my best egg. I dipped it in that red color for so long it looked like a scarlet rose. I sat and stared at that egg for the longest time thinkin' I had created a masterpiece. That's what Momma2 said anyway.

"Well, there, Tilly, you've done made a masterpiece!"

After we finished dyin' all the eggs, Momma2 polished each of them with a rag dipped in bacon grease. It made each of 'em shine like the big chunks of coal we brought in to burn in our old cook stove. My red egg sparkled and shined like a jewel.

When we cleaned up the mess, I took my red egg and hid it under my bed so's no one else could eat on it. I didn't want 'em to destroy that beauty. That's how come I had it for my fishin' day picnic.

I got up early that mornin' and, after we had breakfast, I told Momma2 I was going to head out to fish for a bit. She pretty much let me do whatever I planned 'cuz she wanted me to be independent. She kept tellin' me, "Tilly, you can't depend on anyone else in this world, so ya gotta know how to take care of yourself and be an independent thinker." So, my independent thinkin' mind decided to make my own jelly sandwich. I cut off a couple of slices of Momma2's bread and spread red jelly over each slice. Like I told ya, red's my favorite color. I wrapped the slices in some waxed paper, then I ran to my room and grabbed that egg. I put the egg in the bag and put my sandwich on top of it. I could hardly wait to get to the creek and get to eatin' on that egg.

The creek was down away from the big house along the path Grandpa Poe made when he first built the farmhouse. It had been walked on so much it actually went below ground level. It was wide enough I could skip in it and not trip over the sides. Grasses grew beside it, and 'cuz it was spring, the smell of the earth reached up to my nose and grabbed it makin' me hungry for ever'thing springtime offered. And it offered a lot in our little piece of the world. The Arkansas wildflowers was peekin' their noses out of the ground and color was startin' to come back. I stopped to pick some Indian paintbrush and stick it in my pigtails, pretendin' to be an Indian princess. My mousy brown hair always needed a little sprucin' up and I figured the rich red blooms would add a nice piece a color.

I listened to the birds fill the air with their sounds and stopped to watch a squirrel flit its tail as it looked down at me from a dogwood tree on its way to bloomin'. The squirrel was chatterin' away and was probably tellin' me to get the hell away from his tree.

I knew the legend of the dogwood tree. Ever' time I saw one, its story ran through my head. Zeke told me the story so many times I had it memorized. How it had been used for Christ's cross, then the tree felt so bad 'bout being used for such an awful thing it twisted itself all up. Momma2 said the story was nothing but a bunch of nonsense. She said that a lot about church kind of stuff. Anyway, the blooms weren't out yet, so I didn't pick one and examine it for the cross and crown a thorns. I just kept goin', my cane pole flyin' behind me as I trotted on down the trail.

As I started past the slave house, I decided to stop. Its gray-sloped roof covered a porch that wrapped around the entire place. I climbed onto the porch and put my pole down. The weathered steps was crooked after years of wear and the boards on the house looked like they'd been through hell and back. Tar paper and old cut up pieces of tin plugged holes that kept the mice and the weather out.

Ever' year, Momma2 threatened to tear it down and burn the wood in the stove at the farmhouse, but ever' spring, she'd make her way down and clean it out so it would be ready for any hired help needin' a place to stay while they worked in the orchard.

I went over to the window and looked inside. The grime made it hard for me to see. I rubbed the glass with my hand to make a place for me to peek in. It was dark inside, but I could still see the ol' furniture spread out with memories wrapped around each piece, makin' me ache to get inside and play house. I could see the dust spread over ever'thing like a layer of frost. The door had a padlock on it, and that stopped me gettin' in to mess around a bit, so I took up my pole and headed off.

I could hear the creek 'fore I saw it. It was ragin' with spring run off. Rocks was tumblin' down, and when I got to it, I could see branches from winter storms floatin' away like enormous pickup sticks. Sager Creek had flooded several times, but Grandpa Poe had found our piece of ground that was out of reach of the floodwaters. He'd bought the property back in '25 just 'fore he met Momma2.

The trail threaded all the way down to the creek. My favorite fishin' spot was just past the trail end; it had a rock overhang where I could always catch a big ol' fish or two, or I could just lay on that ol' rock and watch the world go by if'n that's what I wanted to do. Today, I had my mind made up to catch some fish for dinner and eat my red egg.

I loved this time of the year when runoff wasn't finished. It made my trip even more excitin' 'cuz I could throw rocks into the ragin' waters and watch them disappear. The sound of the water wiped out the sound of anything that was movin' around me.

As I walked over to the rock with my pole, I got all transfixed by two dragonflies matin' in the air. Momma2 called it spoonin'. Zeke called it sweepin' the broom. Neither one of 'em made any sense to me. It was plain old matin' as far as I had read, and I had read plenty in Grandpa Poe's old science books.

I learned to read when I was three years old. Momma2 had pulled me up on her lap and spread out a newspaper and showed me how to spell the word *"the"*. Then she and I went through that paper and found every *"the"* we could find. I was proud of myself and Momma2 was just plain over the moon with joy. She looked at me, then grasped my cheeks in her hands and smiled. "You're your momma's baby, Tilly, but you got your Grandpa Poe's brains, Baby Girl. You're gonna be all right."

After that, she spent a little piece of ever' day teachin' me words and the way the letters went together 'til I could put letters together by myself to make words. It didn't take long 'til I could read the *Capper's Weekly* newspaper. It had some good tips in it for farmin' and keepin' up a house. I liked the recipes the best 'cuz when I found a good one, I'd give it to Momma2, and she'd make it. Sometimes I helped her, but most of the time, I just enjoyed the end of it. I could read anything and anything that had words on it was fair game to me.

After throwin' rocks and watchin' the dragonflies finish their business, I took my pole and climbed up on the rock. I hung that old cane pole over the edge of the rock and watched the line dip into the water with one of the fat old worms I had dug up last night. It wasn't long 'til I felt a tug on my line. I pulled for a long time, but the only thing that came up was a snarly old hunk of tree limb. That was the problem with fishin' in early spring—the waters carried too much winter knock down and my pole was always catchin' it.

After the third line pull, I finally netted my first fish. It was a good-sized bullhead. Momma2 would be thrilled to have it for cookin'. I carefully took it off my hook makin' sure I didn't sting myself on the fins. Those fins could hurt like hell if'n you wasn't careful, but Zeke had taught me to be careful, so I was.

After I got it cleaned and packed away in my krill, I went down to the edge of the creek and washed my hands. I wiped 'em on my overalls, took out my brown sack, and set out my picnic food. I admired my beautiful red egg, and even though I didn't want to spoil its beauty by crackin' it, I could hardly wait to eat it. I peeled away that jeweled red shell, and though my nose wasn't favorin' eatin' it, my eyes were, and I ate away. I don't 'member if'n I finished it or not, 'cuz by the end of the day, I was pukin' up sour egg and thinkin' I was gonna to die. Ever' bit of me hurt. My belly hurt, my bones hurt, my eyes even hurt. By the time it was all over, my butt hurt. I can only recall eatin' a bite of my jelly sandwich when I felt the world spinnin' 'round me. My head got all hot and my stomach started to turn over like a pancake on a hot griddle. Zeke found me on the rock, mid-afternoon, when Momma2 sent him out to check on me. Like I said, he found me sicker than a damn dog.

Zeke carried me back to the house. He told Momma2 where he found me. She had him put me on the couch in the front room, and then she took to carin' for me. I could hear her yellin' at Junie Bird to get the slop bucket over to me 'fore I puked all over the house. Junie Bird wasn't good at followin' directions. She got the slop bucket then sat in a chair wringin' her hands and rockin' back and forth, cryin' and wailin' until Momma2 told her to "Shut up and go outside!" Momma2 barely got the slop bucket to me 'fore I started pukin' again. My head felt like an ax had hit it full force.

Pretty soon, I heard the screen door slam shut and heard Junie Bird out on the porch carryin' on like she was the one sick. I could never figure that girl out.

Momma2 brought over a cool rag and washed my forehead and my mouth. That rag felt like Heaven. She asked me what happened, and I told her I didn't know 'cuz I didn't. She fished around for what she needed to know, and when I finally owned up to hidin', then eatin' my favorite Easter egg, she looked at me with big, wide eyes then raised her head to the ceilin' and cried.

"You fool girl, you could kill yourself doing something stupid like that. Whatever were you thinkin'?"

I rarely saw Momma2 cry, so it made me cry too. She only cried when someone she knew died or when she had to kill one of our animals for meat. She was a regular bawler then. But she was cryin' to beat the band, and it was me makin' her cry.

Momma2 yelled out the door for Zeke to run get Doc Gibbs. I felt myself go limp when I heard those words. We didn't call Doc Gibbs for anything. He was the onliest white doctor in Siloam Springs, and Momma2 use to say *"it would have to be an epidemic"* 'fore we had to call Doc Gibbs. I figured I was on my way to meet up with Grandpa Poe.

The outhouse was too far away for me to make a run for it, so I had to use the slop bucket to shit my guts out. I shit so much I thought my stomach was going to come out my butt. Momma 2 kept washin' out the slop bucket gettin' it ready for another round of my sick. She ended up bringin' two slop buckets over—one for my pukin' and one for my shittin'. I was emptying out my body of all kinds of stuff, and none of it smelled like it ever should have been eaten.

When Doc Gibbs came through the door, Junie Bird was hangin' on his arm cryin' like a crazy person. I heard her say, "Tilly gonna die, Docca. She gonna die like a dead person."

Doc Gibbs stroked her hair and patted her arm. "Don't you worry, Miss June, your little girl's gonna be just fine. You just let me have a look at her, will ya?"

Doc took Junie Bird's arm away from his shoulder and led her to a chair where she sat rockin' and wailin'. Momma2 told her to go back out on the porch 'til Doc Gibbs was finished checkin' me over. She must have done that 'cuz I didn't hear her anymore. Then when I started heavin' again, the doctor came rushin' over to hold my head while I threw up the worst tastin' sour I ever had in my mouth. Momma2 held out a cool rag for the doctor, then told him I had eaten an old egg.

I wanted to tell him it was a beautiful egg, but I couldn't bring any words out of me. My body didn't have any energy for talkin'.

He took my temperature, felt around my throat and stomach, then looked up at Momma2. "Miss Lila, Tilly has a bad case of food poisonin'. I don't reckon she'll die, but she's going to feel like it. I don't want her eatin' anything solid for the next two days. Just give her some broth and sweet tea and make sure she drinks plenty of water. Give her a tablespoon of apple cider vinegar ever' hour for the rest of the day and, tomorrow, give her the same dosage in the mornin', at noon, and at bedtime. If you notice her stools gettin' bloody, get her to the hospital. Don't monkey around with that. I'll swing by in a couple of days to see how she's gettin' along. If you need me sooner, just send Zeke over. Right now, she needs to rest, and I don't think you're goin' to be gettin' much rest, Miss Lila, so when she sleeps, you'd better too. And I mean that! Don't be your old stubborn self."

Doc Gibbs got up from the stool he was sittin' on by the couch and patted my head. The cold rag Momma2 had laid there earlier was warm now. "You're gonna be okay Little Tilly, but you're sure not gonna want eggs for awhile."

He tipped his hat to Momma2, picked up his old rugged brown doctor's bag, and headed out the door. I could hear him talkin' to Junie Bird 'fore he left. "Your girl's just fine, Miss June. She just needs to sleep and drink water. Don't you be worryin' any. Tilly's a strong young'un and she'll be up runnin' around in no time. You take care of your Momma. She's going to need your help."

Momma2 brought me a pillow, and I laid my head on the couch arm. "Tilly, you are gonna be the death of me, girl. Whatever gets in your head to do the things you do. An Easter egg of all things! Who would have ever thought to save an Easter egg and then eat the stupid thing?"

I listened to her, but I didn't say anything. I just laid there, and when I needed to, I emptied the part of me that was yellin' to me to get emptied. I felt like my insides was all in those two slop buckets and my head was on fire.

It took more than two days for me to stop being sick. Momma2 emptied and cleaned slop buckets all day and all night. She put blankets down on the floor by the couch and slept right next to me. She fed me broth and sweet tea, and no sooner did I get it down then it would rush right back out of me again. She was lookin' as ragged as the old mop hangin' on the back porch. Her auburn red hair that she favored with brushin' and keepin' shiny laid flat against her head. A matted mess. Her eyes had dark circles and held worry. She was still in the same clothes she had on when Zeke found me.

By the middle of the second day, I finally stopped pukin'. My butt didn't stop shittin' for almost a week. It felt like someone had lit a match and burned a big hole in it.

All the time I was sick, Junie Bird paced back and forth and rocked in her rockin' chair. She hummed and whistled the entire time. That in itself could have made me want to puke or scream, but I knew that was what she did when she had troubles on her mind, so I didn't fuss about it. A couple of times, Momma2 couldn't take it and sent her out on the porch. We could still hear her, but at least it wasn't right in our ears.

Doc Gibbs came by on the third day to check up on me. When he saw Junie Bird by the quiltin' frame, he walked over to see what she was doin'.

"Well now, Miss June, looks to me like you're makin' a mighty fine piece of quiltin'. Who taught you how to do that?

Junie Bird didn't answer him, she just kept on puttin' her needle in and out of the material like her mind was a million miles away, and she couldn't hear anything 'round her. That's how she was. She could get lost in her mind and no one could get in 'til she unlocked her brain. Nobody had the key to it 'cept her. Sometimes she could make you want to scream at her, but it didn't do no good. She'd just start hummin' louder and louder tryin' to drown out your voice. "She was a mystery" was what Momma2 would say. "Your momma's a mystery, Tilly. When she don't want someone in her head, she just plain shuts down her mind."

That's how it was when Doc Gibbs asked her about her quiltin'. She was somewhere in her head, and she wasn't gonna let him in. He patted her head like she was his favorite dog then came over to the couch to see me.

"Well, now, Miss Tilly, how are things goin' for you? Are you ready to be among the livin' again?"

I looked at him and tried my best to smile. That was the easy part. When he started checkin' me over to see how I was doin' I groaned a little when he pushed on my stomach. "Tender, huh?" He asked me and then winked like it was some kind of joke. I personally didn't find it funny at all.

"Yes, Sir," I said. "My stomach feels like Momma2's been butcherin' on it."

He chuckled at that then took my temperature. While he was waitin' for it to read, he spoke to Momma2. "Miss Lila, it's been a long time since I've checked up on you and Miss June. How are y'all doing?"

Momma2 just looked down at him and puzzled up her face a bit. "Why, what on earth do we need checkin' up on? We're fit as fiddles except this here Tilly and her egg business. We don't need anybody checkin' up on us, Doc Gibbs. We take care of ourselves for the most part. Thank you for your kindness."

The doctor took the thermometer out of my mouth makin' me yawn loud. He looked at it for a bit then shook it and put it back in its long tube carrier. "Temperature is normal and her stomach sounds like everything is in workin' order. I want you to give her a piece of garlic for her diarrhea. She might not like the taste of it, but it will calm her bowels. You can start feedin' her some soft foods, then when she acts like she's tired of that, just treat her normal. A couple more days of restin' and she should be as good as new."

Momma2 saw Doc Gibbs to the door, and as he left, she took his arm. "I want to know what your charge is, Will. I don't take things for free—you know that. What do I owe ya?"

The doctor leaned over and placed his bag on the floor. He rubbed his chin like he was thinkin' real hard then picked up his bag. "Miss Lila, I'll be needin' a bushel of red apples in September. I want the sweet kind."

He balanced his bag in his hand and took his hat in the other. "I'll be seein' you, Miss Lila. You take care now."

Chapter 2

I had seven chores to my name. One for ever' year of my life. Zeke and
Momma2 had to do all my chores when I was layin' on the couch sick as a dog.
But now that I was up and at 'em again, the chores was back ta bein' all mine.

First chore I was given was to make my bed ever' mornin' 'fore I stepped
out of my bedroom. My room was the smallest room. It was right off the
kitchen near the back of the house. I had a cot bed that just fit me. At the
end of my little bed Momma2 had stacked a couple apple crates on top a one
another to hold my folded clothes. I didn't have that many clothes; I just
didn't need 'em. I hardly ever had to make a decision about what to wear. I
usually picked out a pair of cutoff overalls and slipped into 'em. I never needed
underwear and it was gettin' warm enough not to even wear a shirt.

On top of my apple crates, Momma2 put a long board to hold my treasures. I had to dust those treasures and sweep my bedroom floor on Saturdays.
They looked right smart at the end of my cot bed. I'd look at my treasures at
night 'fore I dozed off to sleep. My treasure shelf held a couple birds' eggs, a
hummin'bird's nest, and thirty-two Indian arrowheads I found 'round the
farm, and I sure as hell didn't want anybody touchin' my arrowheads 'sides
me. I kept those in three cigar boxes that belonged to Grandpa Poe. I had
cotton stuffed around each arrowhead to keep 'em from gettin' chipped. I
dusted those very careful-like ever' Saturday, and I counted 'em to make sure
Junie Bird's fingers hadn't found 'em.

The quilt on my cot bed was the prettiest thing I owned. Junie Bird had made it for me when she was growin' me in her stomach. It was full of ever' color you could imagine, and it was stuffed with the fluffiest down Momma2 could find. I did love pullin' that ol' quilt over me at night when I snuggled in bed, and I loved pullin' it up and makin' it look all perfect when I got out of bed in the mornin'. It was a good way to end and begin my days. Makin' that quilt was one good thing Junie Bird had done for me, besides makin' me, so I guess I should be grateful, but grateful wasn't what I mostly felt for her. Mostly it was mad.

Ever' mornin', my breakfast was a thick slice of bread smeared with ol' Bossy's butter and Momma2's jam and a cold hard-boiled egg. It took me a few days after I was sick to want to eat an egg again, I can tell you that! Momma2 always poured me a half-cup of coffee, then filled it up with sugar and cream.

A few years ago, I heard Zeke tell Momma2 I was too young to be drinkin' coffee. She just turned her back and said, "She's not too young for anything that's good, Zeke." That ended that.

I had to clean up my own dishes after I ate and had to help dry dinner dishes. Ever' night, I had to collect eggs from the hen house. That was chore number six; then this year, Momma2 added my last and most awful chore. I now had to empty the slop buckets.

Slop buckets was a necessity in our house, but they sure wasn't my favorite thing. The two slop buckets was full of scraps for the pigs, and when they was full, the stink was something terrible. Mostly, they held potato skins and old pieces of bread and some vegetable pieces we didn't eat. Momma2 was good about not givin' the pigs meat or stuff they might not like. She said they had a right to eat good 'fore we ate them. "It was only fair," she said.

She covered the slop buckets with old cracked dishes to keep the stink from fillin' up the house. When Momma2 decided that was gonna be my add-on for my year seven, I nearly went as crazy as Junie Bird.

When I was pitchin' a fit about that new chore, Momma2 looked over at me and turned herself so she was lookin' at me full on. "Mathilda Mae Harris," she said my whole full name not takin' a breath, and I knew I was gonna get a preachin', " Life is full of messes and stink! If you learn to help with something that needs to be done, even if it stinks, then you'll be learnin' a valuable lesson in life. Now, that's your chore, and you're old enough to do it. You do it good, girl!"

I stomped off cryin', but I still had that chore.

The mornin' I learned about chore number seven, I finished my breakfast and put up my dishes. I lifted the lid off the first slop bucket and turned my head to get away from the smell. I had just lifted the second plate cover when I heard Junie Bird comin' at me. I turned just in time to get away.

I'm tellin' ya, Junie Bird is plain gonna run me ragged 'fore I get old enough to tag her down. When she got it in her head that I was gonna play tag with her, off she'd come at me. She'd chase me all around the house gigglin' to beat the band, weavin' in and out of ever' room. I avoided her by passin' under and over pieces of furniture, but she kept runnin' after me yellin', "I's get yous, Tilly, I's get yous."

That day, I wasn't in the mood for her chasin' game, and I made it known to her by yellin' at her to *"Stop chasin' me, Junie Bird—I'm tired of your nonsense!"* But she kept at it.

I could hear her pantin' and laughin' and screechin' as she fired off, "I's gonna catch yous!" over and over.

Me yellin' for her to stop didn't do a bit a good—she just kept at it 'til I ran out of the house. Junie Bird didn't like to go too far away from the house without Momma2 with her, so she quit chasin' me when I passed the ol' red water pump. I turned 'round when she stopped, stuck out my tongue, then turned and wiggled my butt at her.

"Can't get me now, Junie Bird. I done left your imaginary fence, didn't I?" I wiggled my butt again and then took off to tattle.

I found Momma2 on her knees in the garden. The garden was set away from the farmhouse on the other side of the water pump. I could see her with her back bent and a bucket full of weeds beside her. She was pullin' them by hand, her gloved hands rippin' 'em out of the earth like they was a personal pain to her. Her ol' straw hat was sittin' kinda crooked on her head to keep the sun from gettin' on her face. She was fussy about that. She said, "Havin' to work outside all your life is no reason to look like a field hand." So she always covered her face and wore gloves. Of course, Momma2 also wore long pants which no other woman in Benton County I ever saw wore, but she said it made no sense to her to work outside in a dress. Wasn't practical! And, for sure, Momma2 was practical.

There was a pole and wire fence around the garden to keep out most animals that liked the same food we did, but it didn't always keep out the rabbits. Even though the wire had tiny holes in it, they would dig under or squeeze through to get at the food they liked. They was a constant bother, so Momma2 cooked shot rabbit for dinner several times a week durin' the growing season. I liked eatin' the rabbit legs the best. They was skinny and the meat just tore off the bone. Momma2 stewed, fried, and canned rabbit, but we still had plenty of 'em to eat on our garden. I opened the rickety ol' gate to the garden and walked in quietly.

I stood there for a while to let Momma2 know I was there 'fore I tattled on Junie Bird for chasin' me all over kingdom come. Finally, Momma2 told me to stop standin' there and make myself useful. I got down on my knees across the row from her and started pullin' weeds, too.

I think Momma2 and Zeke had taught me ever' single plant name on our property. I knew the weeds, so I pulled those worthless plants out. I threw them in Momma2's bucket, and when I saw it full, I got up and dumped it over the fence so the deer could eat 'em. That's what I think happened anyway. We'd throw out our weeds and the next day they'd be gone. Zeke once told me it was a darn near perfect friendship. We threw out the weeds we didn't want, the deer ate 'em, and then got rid of the seeds so they'd get planted somewhere else. I figured it couldn't be too perfect of a friendship 'cuz that just meant weeds would continue to grow, and then someone would have to pull 'em. Zeke didn't see it that way.

We pulled weeds for nearly an hour 'fore Momma2 started talkin' to me. She liked silent time and thought it was a good habit for me to get into. "Tilly, if you stay quiet long enough, you'll have something to say when it's time to say it. It's good to think more than you talk." She was givin' me practice with that now.

"I suppose we'll plant seed next week."

With a sentence that didn't have any place to go, Momma2 was openin' the way for me to talk.

"Zeke has the orchard started and that leaves me with the garden to get done."

Momma2 always planted a big garden. She had a root cellar a ways down behind the farmhouse, and durin' the fall and winter months, she kept all the potatoes, carrots, beets, onions, and apples she had grown from our orchard down in the cellar so we had vegetables to eat all winter long. All her put-up canned goods was down there too. I hated goin' down in that ol' root cellar on 'count of all the spider webs and dark corners. It was creepy and gave me nightmares. I wasn't fond of holey places.

"Why's Zeke takin' the old tree out down near the pump? That's a good climbin' tree, Momma2."

"There's plenty of good climbin' trees, Tilly. That one's gotta go before a good windstorm takes it out and blows it into our house. It'll be good firewood for the stove."

"Grandpa Poe's Eve tree is getting old. How come Zeke isn't choppin' it down?"

Grandpa Poe had planted the Eve tree the first day he bought the farm, so it was old, and I do mean old. It was twisted and knotted in so many places that it looked like a gnarled up ol' man. It was named the Eve tree on account a it was the first tree Grandpa Poe planted. It was planted near the slave house and looked like it could come crashing down any day. Ever' year Momma2 went down to check to see if it would produce leaves and ever' year it did, so she kept it just for her Grandpa Poe.

"That tree don't come down 'til I do, Tilly. That's your Grandpa's tree. It don't hurt nobody, and it isn't in nobody's way down there. Makes a nice shade for the summer help. "Sides that, Tilly, that ol' tree stands for love. You love what you plant, and you tend to it for all it needs. Just 'cuz it's old, don't mean it don't have purpose. Your Grandpa Poe planted that tree, and he loved it. The Eve tree stands for love, Tilly, it don't come down 'til its end!"

I'd already known she'd say something like that 'cuz I'd heard her say it so many times, but it didn't seem right for my best climbin' tree to get cut down and that ol' tree could still stand.

Momma2 tried to distract me from the climbin' tree by quizzin' me about some of the weed names. Then it wasn't long 'fore I couldn't help myself on the tattlin' part.

"Momma2, Junie Bird is gonna be the end of me if'n she don't change her habits of chasin' me when she gets to bein' in her silliness. She just won't listen to me."

"Well, Tilly, Junie Bird doesn't get much fun in her life. I don't think a little chasin' is gonna hurt you any. Gives her a bit of laughter, doesn't it? Sure doesn't hurt anyone to give 'em a little of that, now does it?"

Momma2 didn't understand me and Junie Bird. Junie Bird was always pesterin' me and no matter how much I wanted to, I couldn't get away from her bein' in the way of me. She just plain vexed me more often than she was suppose to.

Momma2 kept on pullin' weeds movin' down the row as she did. When she came to the end of the row, she got up slowly and put her hands on her knees bendin' over slightly as she did. The gray plaid shirt she wore must of belonged to Grandpa Poe 'cuz it hung almost to her knees. Then she quietly said to me, "Tilly, you need to give your Momma a little forgiveness. She doesn't mean any harm in what she does. She just doesn't know any better."

That was what I had grown up hearin' all my life. "Your momma just doesn't know any better." I was gettin' pretty sick and tired of that excuse. She was older than me, and she was *my* momma. She should get to knowin' better! But she didn't. She was dumber than a pile of rocks as far as I could see.

Momma2 threw her weeds over the fence for the deer, then started walkin' back to the house. I didn't hesitate to follow her—anything to get out of pullin' more of those damn weeds.

As we walked back, I couldn't help but notice the farmhouse looked brand spankin' new, 'cuz Momma2 had had Zeke whitewash it durin' the time the orchard was dry. He did whatever Momma2 told him to. As a matter of fact, she bossed all of us around.

When we got near the pump, Momma2 stopped and started pumpin' water for us to drink. We bent over to let the fresh, clear water run down our throats and whet our thirst. "It was the best taste in the whole wide world!" is what Momma2 would say.

She pumped while I drank my fill, then she took off her hat and wiped her forehead with the dark blue handkerchief she had tied 'round her neck to keep the sweat from runnin' down her shirt.

"You got chores to get done, young lady, 'fore you go out for the day. Go get 'em done."

That was her way of endin' our time together, and I pretty much knew she wasn't gonna listen to me anymore about Junie Bird.

Momma2 had chores, too. She was busy from sunup to sundown. She didn't *"let grass grow under her feet,"* as she always said. I wasn't suppose to either.

As I walked back into the house to get the slop buckets, I peeked around the corner to see where Junie Bird was. She was sittin' by the cold stove with a quilt on her lap, sewin' and hummin'. I knew I was safe. When she was sewin' and hummin', nothing could disturb her mind.

As I walked past Junie Bird, the sun, comin' through the east window, was shinin' on her like she was some kinda holy angel. She looked like a regular normal person just sittin' there makin' a beautiful quilt. I didn't get lucky gettin' her hair. Mine was just plain brown. She had hair the color of cream. And she had a lot of it. It usually hung down her back, but sometimes, Momma2 would plait it in a long braid, and today, that's how it was. The braid wrapped around her shoulder and fell down the front of her dress like a python snake. Her eyes, the color of a hazelnut, was fixed on her needle as it threaded itself in and out of the material she was workin'. Momma2 was always tellin' her she was her beautiful daughter, and it was the plain truth—Junie Bird was dumber than snot, but she was beautiful.

I walked like a sneaky Indian past her, picked up the slop buckets, and headed outside. The pigs could hear me comin' with that stinky slop bucket. As soon as I got near their pen, they started squealin' so loud you'd think they was gettin' killed. The big boar pig was the noisiest and rushed over to the trough to get his share first. I named him Rude. The sow, who I called Puck 'cuz, she always seemed like she was full of it, was fat and full of piglets, so her hurry didn't amount to very fast, but she eventually got there. As soon as she did, she pushed her way into her share of the slop.

The pigpen rested near the big barn and held a mud bath and shelter. Grandpa Poe had built the fence and pen 'fore I was born, and it was still standin' good and solid even though it was weather worn.

Momma2 freshened up the straw on the ground for the pigs ever' other day, but the pigs managed to stir it in their mud bath quicker than you could yell "bacon." They just plum loved to muck around in that dirty water and smear it all over themselves. Made you wonder about eatin' 'em, dirty as they was.

After I poured the slop bucket into their food, I had to wash it out usin' the spigot on the barn, then bring it back into the house to get filled up again. The mess of life was a never-ending circle.

Grandpa Poe and Zeke had built ever' buildin' on the farm 'cept the slave house. It was already there when he bought the land. The barn was the biggest thing on the land 'cuz it had the biggest job. It held all the orchard tools and the crates that carried the apples off to market in late September. The orchard workers had to bring all the apples to the barn to store in the bins for separatin', and then, Zeke lived in the barn, too, so it needed to be big. It wasn't painted red like all the other barns. Zeke just put linseed oil on it with lime, so it looked like leather. I loved the smell of the barn 'cuz it always held the sweetness of fresh apples in its air.

Ol' Bossy cow and her calf were in the pasture behind the barn. I didn't have any chores with them, but I loved to go over and watch 'em stand together and chew on grass. The calf was pretty new and stayed close to ol' Bossy. They was both roan colored. We didn't own a bull. We borrowed one whenever ol' Bossy needed a calf. Momma2 said bulls was *too darn mean.*

"Darn" was 'bout the worst word I ever heard Momma2 say. She didn't use bad words. She repeated over and over, "If you have a good use of the English language, you don't need to use *'those'* words". My mind couldn't help it. I personally loved the sound of bad words, and I knew all of 'em. Orchard hands had used 'em ever since I could hear and understand 'em, and my head learned to use 'em in my thinkin'. They just seemed to fit my independent mind, and Momma2 didn't have to hear my thoughts.

When I finished with the slop buckets, I climbed up on the hay bales near the barn and took my time watchin' ol' Bossy and her calf. I pulled a couple of stems of hay out to stick in my mouth to suck on while I watched her lick her calf. The calf dove under her big ol' belly to get at the milk we shared with it. Momma2 milked ol' Bossy ever' night 'fore she went to bed. Then she'd bring the milk in and put it in the separator to be ready for our next mornin's breakfast.

We got *this* ol' Bossy from a neighbor down the road last year. She was some kind of special milkin' cow, and Momma2 was kickin' up her heels when we got her. We had had other ol' Bossys, but this one was the newest. The others either died of old age or died of some disease. She was the third ol' Bossy since I could remember.

I couldn't help think that ol' cow was a better momma to her calf than Junie Bird was to me. Ol' Bossy wasn't pesterin' her calf all day by chasin' her all over the pasture. That ol' cow knew better, that was for sure.

Chapter 3

Our truck bounced down the road. Junic Bird and me was squealin' like
Rude, our ol' boar. Junie Bird had her hands in the air lettin' the wind fly
through 'em like they was kites. She had her head up whoopin' and hollerin'.
I watched her and squealed along with her findin' myself laughin' at her
laughin'. Even though she was lots older, she was as young as me in her mind.

The truck was an ol' red 1950 Chevy. Momma2 bought it when I was 5
years old. 'Fore that, she only drove Grandpa Poe's ol' Model A Ford pickup.
Zeke still drove that ol' thing around the orchard to help carry tools and stuff.
That ol' Model A *really* bounced when you rode in the back. Junie Bird was
wild about gettin' to go in it.

We lived 11 miles from Siloam Springs, and it took us ever' bit of twenty
minutes to get there. The orchard grew right along the road that led us straight
into town, and I loved lookin' down the rows of trees as we rode past it.

The road to Siloam Springs was rutted from all the drivin' on the wet
dirt. Sometimes it took a great deal of hold on to keep inside the back of the
truck when we was sittin' in it.

We usually had to go to town once a week to get groceries, and that was the
most excitin' day of the week! 'Sides Junie Bird and me, the back of the truck
held two ol' boxes for Zeke and Momma2 to fill with whatever we picked
up in town. They used the boxes 'til they broke down and then Momma2
burned 'em. These two boxes was in pretty good shape, and I figured they'd

be good for several more trips. One of the boxes held close to three-dozen eggs all wrapped up in soft hay. These was the extra eggs we didn't use for the week, and Momma2 traded 'em at the general store for stuff she needed. The grocer, Mr. Tribble, always liked Momma2's eggs 'cuz they didn't have rooster blood in 'em. He was particular about that. He was a particular man 'bout lots of things. He kept his store real tidy and neat lookin' with everythin' in its place. He wore a bowtie that fit tight 'round his neck, and his shirt and pants always looked like they just got off the ironin' board. He couldn't do much for his hair, 'cuz there was none there, but he shined his top like it was a crystal ball ready to be looked at. He had glasses that layed on his nose, so's he could look up from his money tickets or look ya straight in the eye. He was good at that part. He kept his eyes on everythin' and ever'one in his store. He was a particular man.

As we drove toward his store, the countryside passed by us as we flew down the road like a snake whippin' by. Houses was stuck here and there. Sager Creek was hid behind 'em, but I knew it was there runnin' with wild water. Some of the houses was on poor land that barely made anything grow, and they always looked like they was beggin' to be better than they was. One of those houses belonged to the Putters. They lived in the house where Zeke use' to live 'fore he had bad times and had to move to Grandpa Poe's place. The Putters was what Momma2 called *"low people."*

The Putter yard was the worst. They had trees that was beggin' for water and care, and their house was barely put together. Their yard was always full of throwaway stuff they never put away. The Putters made dirt look ugly! Momma2 use' ta frown whenever she talked about 'em. "Nobody needs to be trashy just 'cuz they're poor. Poor shouldn't make lazy come alive. Poor should make you fight to do better. They are just plain low people."

No matter how she felt about the Putters, it didn't stop Momma2 from hiring their Putters' twin boys the last two summers to work in the orchard during the apple season. They was strong workers and needed the money. Momma2 said she didn't think they ever' saw any of it 'cuz their daddy drank it all up. I didn't like havin' 'em around. They always called Zeke boy, like he was younger than they was, and even though Momma2 had given 'em a piece of her mind when she heard 'em, they still did it when she wasn't 'round.

Zeke didn't put up a fuss about name callin'. He just said, "Those boys don't have nobody to show 'em any better."

Seemed to me they didn't need nobody to show 'em Zeke weren't a boy. He was a man full grown with grayin' hair and whiskers growin' around his face. I loved his brown skin and use' to ask him if I could rub some of his brown on to my white to make myself a better color. He use' to tussle my hair and say, "Why, Miss Tilly, you don't need none of ol' Zeke's brown color. You's the best color in all of Arkansas."

When I was too little to ride in the back of the truck, I would sit up in the front with Momma2 and Zeke and listen to 'em tell stories about the people on the road. That's how I come to know about Zeke's bad time.

Zeke's momma and daddy was slaves. That meant someone owned 'em like we owned ol' Bossy. I never could quite see how that all worked, and I, for sure, was glad Zeke didn't have to be a slave to nobody. He was born a free darkie. After the war, Zeke's momma and daddy worked as sharecroppers. He worked with his folks on their piece of land 'til he was twenty, then he moved to the place near us where the Putters live now. That place belonged to an ol' white man named Blair who was partial to darkies. After Zeke worked for him for seven years, ol' man Blair told Zeke he could buy the house and the acre around it. Zeke worked for the next three years, saved his money, and went to ol' Blair. The land belonged to Zeke.

Zeke's house was down near Sager Creek in the low land, and even though it was hard to farm, Zeke worked hard and made it grow sweet potatoes that he sold to ol' man Blair who sold 'em to the whites in town, since some whites wouldn't buy from darkies 'cuz they thought they was low people like the Putters. Zeke wasn't a low people at all, and I bet his sweet potatoes was the best in the country.

Zeke made his land work through the first two years and married Belva going into the third. When Sager Creek flooded in '26, he had to find work to help him survive. That's when he and Grandpa Poe became friends. That's how Zeke tells it anyway.

Grandpa Poe bought our place in '25 and was livin' in the slave house tryin' to build the barn and the house. Zeke came and helped him with the buildin' durin' the day. He left Belva in the low land at their house and walked up the road to work at Grandpa Poe's. They worked side by side and sometimes, Zeke said, "That ol' Poe could spend the whole day workin' and not say a word. Just think the day away." Maybe that's why Momma2 wanted me to get acquainted with quiet time.

Zeke's Belva died tryin' to have their little baby girl. They was way out in the woods, and no white doctor would come to help her. All the darkies that could help lived on the other side of Siloam, so they couldn't get there in time. She died with her body twisted up in pain. She worked hard to get that baby out alive, but they both was too tired to live. Zeke's eyes were wet whenever he talked about that.

Zeke asked Grandpa Poe if he could bury Belva and his baby girl on Grandpa Poe's land where the water couldn't get at 'em. That's how come Belva and his baby girl are buried in our cemetery. Grandpa Poe's the only other one there.

Zeke couldn't bear to live in his house without Belva, so he sold his place to the Putters and moved into the barn on Grandpa Poe's place. That was near on thirty years ago, and he's been here ever since.

When Grandpa Poe met Momma2 at Siloam Springs Library, it was a love happenin' thing. Momma2 had her head in a book studyin' when Grandpa Poe sat down at her table. She looked up, smiled, and then went back ta studin'. She said she could feel Grandpa Poe starin' at her, and, finally, she put down her book and asked him what the matter was? Grandpa Poe said, "My name's Poe Harris. Excuse my starin. I never seen a redheaded woman before and a pretty one at that."

Momma2 always smiles when she tells that story.

Grandpa Poe use to go to the library to read all the books he could on plantin' and growin' and farmin'. Momma2 always says, "Your Grandpa Poe was some smart man."

Momma2 said Grandpa Poe showed up at the library ever' time she was there. and 'fore long he asked her to go to a movie. After that, they spent all their time together, and when the summer came and Momma2 had finished her second year of college, her family from Fayetteville came down to Siloam

Springs, and Momma2 and Grandpa Poe got married. They moved into the new farmhouse Grandpa Poe and Zeke built with their very own hands.

Now that Grandpa Poe was in the earth, Momma2 visited him, right regular, down at his restin' spot.

"My Poe." That's what she called him when she went out to the cemetery to talk to him. I've heard her talkin' to him like he was right there, sittin' beside her, hearin' ever' word she said. "My Poe, " she'd say, then she'd just have a regular ol' conversation. Couldn't for the life of me know why she did that.

After they was married, Momma2, Grandpa Poe, along with Zeke planted the apple orchard next to the big barn. Grandpa Poe grew apples, and Momma 2 grew her garden. When Momma2 started growin' Junie Bird in her belly, Grandpa Poe was silly happy. That's what Momma2 said anyway. "Your Grandpa Poe was silly happy when we had Junie Bird."

Grandpa Poe and Momma2 didn't care if Junie Bird wasn't made whole. They just plain loved her. Momma2 never had any more babies after Junie Bird 'cuz I'm guessin' Junie Bird was just about enough for 'em. Most of the time I was thinkin' she was one too many for me. But today, when we was ridin' to town, I was likin' her.

When we pulled up to the General Store, town was busy with people on the sidewalk. After Momma2 parked the truck, the dust from the road began settlin' down. Zeke could drive, but he could never drive us to town. No one wanted to see an uppity darkie drivin' a truck with white people in it. Zeke waited until Momma2 got out of the truck, then he got out and lifted me out of the truck. Junie Bird could climb out by herself. We all followed Momma2 inside the store. Zeke was carryin' the box of eggs with his head down and walkin' behind all of us. He did that 'cuz he didn't want people to think he was same as us, but he was.

Mr. Tribble was behind the counter. "Well, good mornin' to y'all, Miss Lila. You're lookin' like spring is fixin' to be good to ya."

Momma2 nodded to him and smiled, but she didn't say anything; she just walked over to the shelves and started takin' down what she needed. Junie Bird went over to the candy bin and started cooing like a bird. That's how she got her name Junie Bird. When she was little she didn't start talkin' like a normal person, but she cooed like a bird to make her sounds. Grandpa Poe called her his "Junie Bird" and it stuck.

Momma2 came over to the bin and told Junie Bird and me to pick out two pieces of candy each. Junie Bird always went for the licorice and peppermint sticks. I tried something new ever' time, and this time, I decided to try horehound candy and butterscotch. The minute I put that horehound candy in my mouth, I knew I made a big mistake! It was plumb awful. The minute it hit my tongue, my face turned up with a sore look. I knew I had to finish it 'cuz there was no wastin' in Momma2's mind. I decided the only way I could get rid of the thing was to chew it down and swallow the terrible taste as fast as I could. I thought I was goin' be sick from it. When the butterscotch hit my mouth, I celebrated the sweet good taste of it. It was better than anything! I decided, right there and then, I wouldn't be tryin' anything new again. I never ever wanted ta risk gettin' anything like that horehound taste in my mouth ever again.

As we was finishin' up our business with Mr. Tribble, Mrs. Malcolm and her two girls came into the store. She was married to Mr. Malcolm, the boss at the bank. Mrs. Malcolm and her daughters was always dressed to beat the band. That's what Momma2 called "gettin' fancy dressed." They was wearin' store-bought dresses that had so much lace and frill they looked like the girls in the catalogs that the mailman brought to our house. I could tell them dresses wouldn't be no good for playin'. They was just sittin' or goin' ta town dresses and that was where they was right now, pokin' around the store, whisperin' and staring at us when Junie Bird decided to act like her crazy self. With a peppermint stick stuck in her mouth, Junie Bird was staring up at the ceilin' like there was somethin' there nobody else could see and pointin' at it. She started in hummin' her hummin' sound and flippin' her arms in the air like she was gonna fly off somewhere. Mrs. Malcolm's girls stopped what they was doin' and started gigglin' at her. They made laughin' *sound* like a mean thing. I looked over at 'em and gave 'em a look that should have stopped their nonsense, but they just kept goin'. Even Mrs. Malcolm had a smile on her face that I knew was not a friendly smile, but one that was laughing at Junie Bird, too. The Malcolm girls got into a gigglin' fit over Junie Bird's hummin' and flappin'. Momma2 was ignorin' 'em, but they was makin' my blood feel like it was burnin' in my body. Zeke put his hand on my shoulder, but that didn't cool me down none. I looked over to 'em and put my hands on my hips. The words started out of me 'fore I knew they was comin'. "What in hell's name are you laughin' at, you silly fools?" I didn't even know I said "hell" out loud—it just came from my mind to my mouth without permission.

Momma2 took my face in her hand and turned me 'round so she was lookin' at me straight in the eyes.. "Tilly!" She said my name in such a quiet voice it took me a second to hear her. She said it again, drawing it out to make sure I was lookin' at her. "Till...eee, you owe Mrs. Malcolm and her girls an apology. Get busy with it, now!"

My forehead made a frown line that went deep in my skin as I turned back to the two fool girls. "They was laughin' at Junie Bird, Momma2!"

I still had my hands on my hips and was ready to fight 'em. Momma2 turned my head back to face her. Her face was red like I never saw it before. "Tilly, I mean what I say, girl! You apologize to Mrs. Malcolm and her daughters, or you and me are goin' outside and it's not goin' to fare well for ya."

Mrs. Malcolm and her girls were quiet and was starin' at me now. Mr. Tribble and Zeke had their heads down tryin' not to get involved in what was happenin'.

My breath came out of my body like ol' Bossy's breath on a frosty mornin'. I looked over at Junie Bird hummin', then turned to Mrs. Malcolm and those girls "dressed to beat the band." I took another breath as Momma2 squeezed on my shoulder to remind me to get goin'.

As fast as my tongue could work, I said, "I'm sorry I said 'hell' out loud!" I turned and ran out of the store whippin' Momma2's hand off my shoulder 'fore anyone could say a word. I climbed in the back of the truck and put my head in my lap. I didn't want to see any of 'em. Not Momma2, not Zeke, and for sure not Junie Bird. I was done with town for the day. So much for my "best day of the week!"

Chapter 4

I was out in the henhouse pickin' up eggs when Momma2 came in. I hadn't talked all the way home from Siloam Springs, and I wasn't plannin' on talkin' again for a long, long time.

I heard Momma2 step inside, but I ignored her. She started talkin' to the chickens like they was actually listenin' to her. She clucked and made chicken noises, pickin' up eggs as she did. She put 'em in the basket I had set on the hen rack and kept on makin' noises' 'til pretty soon she started talkin' like I should be listenin'. My eyes stared straight ahead. I was bound and determined not to look over at her.

"Tilly, not ever'one understands your momma. She's a wonder, and I know it's hard on you. I don't s'pect you to understand the whole of it, but she's your momma, and you're gonna have to deal with that for a long time to come."

I knew the story of my momma and me 'cuz Momma2 didn't believe in keepin' any secrets. I grew up hearin', *"Tilly, you wasn't exactly what I bargained for, but you're everything I ever wanted."*

When Junie Bird was 14 years old, a new preacher man had driven out to the farm to introduce himself. He was drivin' a big ol' blue Buick and was wearin' a blue suit that was wrinkled from bein' in the car. The preacher man didn't have no whiskers on his face and looked too young to be preachin'. He had bushy brown hair that seemed wild and out of control. Momma2 said his hair looked like it had a mind of its own.

Grandpa Poe told him they had enough religion and didn't need none of what he was sellin', but the preacher was a smilin' man and seemed fresh with the word, so Momma2 invited him to stay for supper, somethin' she'd-a-done for any stranger to the farm, so he stayed.

They talked, then laughed, and he came by the next week just to say "hey." The preacher man stayed for supper three times, then on the fourth time he came by the house, he asked if he could take Junie Bird to church the followin' Sunday. Junie Bird didn't get any invites to go places, so Momma2 thought it might be good for her to go and be with others. After all, she thought, *"Your Grandpa Poe and me aren't gonna be around forever."*

Wasn't long and Junie Bird was goin' to church ever' Sunday. Preacher man was prompt to pick her up and prompt to deliver her back to the farm. The only trouble came when Junie Bird started talkin' 'bout bein' filled with the Holy Ghost.

"I's get Hoey Gust," she'd say to Momma2 and Grandpa Poe ever' time she'd come back from church. Junie Bird didn't have a lot of words, but when she'd get some, she could plumb wear ya' out with sayin' 'em over and over. Momma2 said she nearly drove her and Grandpa Poe crazy with her, "Hoey Gust," so when she started saying it over and over, Momma2 would hug her and give her a smile then go off to do her house work, trying to ignore her best she could.

Grandpa Poe was not happy about all the church goin'. He was gettin' tired of the preacher man comin' ever' week for dinner and drivin' up to pick up Junie Bird. Seemed like ever' time he came that ol' preacher man would have to have a word of prayer, and Momma2 and Grandpa Poe wasn't the prayin' kind. They was respectful, and they was glad that Junie Bird was gettin' out to see folks other than themselves, but there was just so much of the churchin' stuff they could handle.

Then when a Sunday came and went that the preacher man didn't show up, they figured he was sick or somethin' and went on with the week with no more thinkin' about him. The next week when Momma2 and Grandpa Poe went to town for their weekly trip, Mr. Tribble asked if Miss Junie Bird was okay. That was a curious question to 'em, so they asked what he was talkin' about. When Mr. Tribble realized they didn't know what was goin' on with the preacher man, he bowed his head low and tried to take care of their business without sayin' anything else. That didn't work 'cuz Grandpa Poe was too smart for that. He said, "Darn it, Tribble, what in God's name you talkin' about. Why should anything be wrong with Junie Bird? She's sittin' in the darn Ford outside, waitin' for us."

I'm thinkin', when I hear the story, that Grandpa Poe didn't say *"darn."*

Mr. Tribble clearly didn't want to tell Grandpa Poe and Momma2 why he was worrin' over Junie Bird, so he just says, "Well, you know how friendly that preacher man was with the girls." He said it like Grandpa Poe and Momma2 should-a-known somethin' they didn't. Mr. Tribble continued, "Mac McConnelly run him out of town a couple weeks back 'cuz he found him bein' too friendly with his daughter. Guess he was too friendly with all the girls."

Grandpa Poe and Momma2 just looked at one another. Momma2 said she didn't know how Grandpa Poe's stomach felt, but hers felt sick when she heard that. Momma2 told me, "Your Grandpa Poe didn't talk for a week after that conversation."

The preacher man never did come back for Junie Bird, but he didn't have to—he left a piece of himself inside her and it grew me. Junie Bird had no idea what was happenin' to her body. Her body made me all by itself. When Momma2 realized her baby was growin' a baby, she told Grandpa Poe. She said it was the only time she ever saw him cry. She told me this story like it belonged to me and I guess it did. But I remember it making me a little sad knowin' my comin' made Grandpa Poe cry.

She told Grandpa, "What's done is done, Poe. Our girl's havin' a baby, and it looks to me like its gonna come with us wantin' it to happen or not." Grandpa Poe never did get to see me born. Zeke found him layin' in the apple orchard the next day. Grandpa Poe's body was bent over a wheelbarrow, gray and cold. Zeke picked up Grandpa Poe's body and carried him like a baby back to Momma2's house. Momma2 said when she saw him comin' with Grandpa Poe in his arms, she ran like the wind to see what the matter was. She said she wanted to die right there and then, but she had business on this earth to take care of, and she had to get to it. It didn't stop her from missin'

Grandpa Poe somethin' terrible though. I still catch her cryin' at his grave sometimes when she's down there talkin' to *her Poe*.

Doc Gibbs said Grandpa Poe's heart gave out on him. Momma2 said it just plumb broke in half.

Together, Zeke and Momma2 dug Grandpa Poe's grave. Momma2 said she was so mad at the world, she threw ever' shovel of dirt with power she didn't know she had. But that didn't stop Grandpa Poe from being dead, and that didn't stop me from being born.

Grandpa Poe was buried right next to Zeke's wife, Belva, and their baby girl. It looked like a regular family layin' there in the cemetery. It weren't regular at all. But the people who loved 'em was able to visit 'em regular, and that was a comfort to 'em.

Zeke built a sittin' bench beside Grandpa Poe's headstone, so Momma2 could visit him when she wanted to. And she did that right regular.

Five months after Grandpa Poe was buried, Doc Gibbs came out to help Junie Bird give birth to me. I've seen the sow and ol' Bossy have their young, so I know its not a comfortable thing, but I guess from Momma2's story, Junie Bird thought something awful was happenin' to her, and there was no way to explain to her what it was. Momma2 said Doc Gibbs finally had to give her a powerful medicine to put her to sleep 'til it was all over. Momma2 said I traded places on this earth with Grandpa Poe, and I gave her another reason to live.

I wasn't feelin' like I gave her a reason to live right now in the henhouse, I was feelin' pretty much like I wanted to be left alone by myself. But she kept talkin'.

"Tilly, not much use me tellin' you how to feel about your momma. Junie Bird is gonna make your life a lot more complicated than it should be." Momma2 paused, and I could hear her take a breath to keep goin'.

"You know, Tilly, it's a funny thing about these hens here. They just drop their eggs and don't think nothin' about it. Ever' one of 'em could be a livin' thing, but they just put 'em out of their bodies and don't pay 'em any mind. But, you let one of these ol' hens sit on their nest and start broodin', and it's harder than blazes to get to their eggs from underneath 'em."

"That's not the kinda momma you got, Tilly. Junie Bird really don't know she's gotta momma you. She just thinks you're some kinda play toy for her. She never got the momma message. But you, Tilly, you are as smart as your Grandpa Poe. You are gonna' get a chance to do things your momma will never do, and, Tilly, you listen to me now, girl."

Momma2 took a deep breath after she told me to "listen, girl," and it seemed to me she was gettin' brave to say somethin' more.

"You're gettin' older and you can see how your momma's different than others. I wish you could always see her through little girl eyes, but that's not the way of the world. You gotta know what's real. And the real thing is, people won't ever see your momma like I see her or Zeke sees her or you see her. Sometimes, like today, people will see Junie Bird like she should be laughed at or teased. Some people will try to take advantage of your momma, Tilly, and it's up to us to keep her safe."

I got all confused then 'cuz in my mind I was doin' just that with those uppity town girls when I asked 'em why they was laughin' at Junie Bird.

Momma2 kept on goin'. "I know you was tryin' to make those girls stop seeing Junie Bird as strange, but they aren't as smart as you. I made you apologize 'cuz I never want you to put yourself in a low place with others and cussin' at 'em put you there. I was proud of you for standing up for your momma, Tilly. I was right proud of you. But you can't say those kind of words to people. I want you better than they are."

I never heard Momma2 say the word "proud" before. That word stayed in my head for a minute before I started to cry. Momma2 came over and sat down beside me on the hen rack. She put my head in her lap and began patting my head softly.

"I know, baby girl. I know. You shouldn't have to momma your momma, but that's how it's gonna be. I'll help you long as I live. You just gotta do it the right way."

We stayed like that for a long time in that henhouse. She kept pattin' my head, and I kept cryin'. I cried and cried. When I finally didn't have any more tears left in me, I wiped my nose with the back of my hand and looked up at Momma2. Her face was wet and streaked with tears. I finally pulled away and stood up and just stared at her. She took the bottom of her shirt and wiped away my tears. She took the basket of eggs, put her hand on my shoulder, and hugged me with her eyes. We walked out of the henhouse together. We walked over to the cows and I stood beside her to watch as she milked ol' Bossy. We each let the whispers in the air surround us. We was both needin' quiet time.

When Momma2 was finished with the milkin', she picked up the bucket of frothy milk and reached for my hand. I took her hand, lettin' it wrap me in its warmth. We walked back to the house. My head and my heart was listenin' to and tryin' to hear what Momma2 was tryin' to tell me.

Chapter 5

I saw the dust and heard the car when I was out in the orchard followin' Zeke around. I ran to see who was comin' to see us. I left Zeke to do his work. This was a busy time of year for apple trees. He was cuttin' limbs to make the trees grow right, and he was always fussin' with the dirt to make sure it was turned to let water flow around the trees and let the air get into the roots. There was more thinkin' to growin' apples than I cared to think about. But Zeke was the best grower, and our apple trees grew the biggest and best apples.

Zeke learned apple tree growin' from Grandpa Poe, and Grandpa Poe learned it from readin' books. Grandpa Poe wasn't a natural born farmer is what Momma2 said, but he was a natural born learner, and he learned what he wanted to know about growin' apples in Arkansas. Zeke learned right along with him.

They planted twenty young apple trees the first year Zeke came to work with Grandpa Poe. Ten Hawkeye red delicious and ten Arkansas Black. Just like everythin' else, it took two different kinds to make apples, and these two kinds was the kinds Grandpa Poe wanted to grow. He planted white-blossomed crab apple trees in the middle of each row to help do the job.

Each year they added a few new trees so's that the orchard would never get too old and always had somethin' new growin'. Momma2 was use to the orchard work and knew how to do everythin' there was to do, but it was Zeke who done it all. Momma2 took care of the bossin'. And she was really good at that!

Zeke was in the middle of prunin' the trees so the ol' dried and dead branches and limbs was out of the way so the sun could get in and *kiss on the leaves.* That's what ol' Zeke told me. He was always sweatin' and workin'. I could hear him cuttin' away and sometimes I saw him stick an ol' clothespin in his mouth gettin' ready to push it on to a young limb to steer its growth the way Zeke thought it needed to go.

I just busied myself with runnin' around pretendin' I was a damn injun ready to scalp all the white people comin' to take this land. My mind would run wild in the orchard chasin' by myself. Peekin' 'round trees, scarin' myself silly sometimes when my imagination got the best of me, or I heard a funny noise or saw a shadow I didn't rightly know.

Today, I heard that car noise and went runnin' to the front of the yard to see what it was bringin' in. The first thing I saw was a red flashy car with shiny wheels and a hood that folded down so the hair on the head of two women was flyin' around in the air like a tornado. For a minute, I couldn't believe my eyes. I stopped and stared at it as it drove up to the house and stopped.

I watched as the woman drivin' leaned over to whisper somethin' to the other one then the driver got out of the car and started walkin' up to Momma2's door. She didn't make it very far 'cuz Momma2 was out of the door and Junie Bird was right behind her. I could see Junie Bird was curious, but she stayed behind Momma2 waitin' to see what was happenin'. Momma2 had her usual flour sack apron 'round herself and was liftin' it up and wipin' her hands as she come out the door.

"What y'all needin' here?" I heard Momma2 ask and I noticed her way of askin' wasn't too friendly.

The driver came forward with her hand out. She was kinda' big accordin' to Momma2's and Junie Bird's size, but fat wouldn't be what I'da called her. But she weren't little neither. Her hair was cut real short, and it had a wave 'round her ears like it was meant to stay that way. I liked the color of her hair 'cuz it was black like Zeke's, but she wasn't no darkie. She was the only other lady 'sides Momma2 I ever saw wear pants, and hers was new lookin' and so was her shoes. When you don't get to see a lot of people, you notice things when you do, and I was noticin' her real good.

I noticed Momma2 didn't take the new lady's hand. She just put down her apron and looked at her waitin' for the driver lady to answer the question Momma2 asked her. The lady with the pants put her hand down real slow-like and looked at Momma2 straight in the eyes.

"Mrs. Harris, my name's Katherine Margaret Murphy, that's my sister, Essie Lou. People call me Kate."

I knew right off, the minute the words came out her mouth, she was a Yankee full-blown. Wondered even more what a Yankee would be doin' down in Arkansas in the middle of our place. Maybe sellin' somethin', but it didn't seem likely.

"Mr. Tribble, back in Siloam, told me you look for workers for your orchard from time to time, and I'm lookin' for work. I spent my young years on a farm in New York, so I know what to do with an orchard, and I'm a good hand. I've been in Philadelphia for the past 10 years working in a packing shed with my sister. They laid us off, and now I'm wanting to find a place to stay that is quiet for Essie Lou. She had an accident and isn't talking any more. She can do housework for you, and she is a real good cook. She hand sews and can do anything you need to help you out. We'd work for room and board and gas and spending money. We don't need much. We're honest, and you won't be sorry if you take us on."

I was listenin' to her thinkin' she had a whole lot of words to get a job. Momma2 picked up her apron again. "What kinda accident did your sister have?"

Momma2 had a sneaky look in her eye when she asked that question. I'd seen that sneaky eye before and I knew for sure that was it.

"Well, ma'am, it's one I'm not comfortable telling you about, but it was a bad accident. I don't want her remembering it, and I don't want her to hear me tell you."

That lady looked like it pained her to give that answer, but her lips were closed tight after that. Momma2 picked up her apron and wiped at her hands again. She looked over at the car then over at the driver lady standin' outside.

"That's a pretty fancy car to have down here on a farm, you might know that, but I thought you should know it won't come in handy for anything I might have you do. You could sell it for somethin' practical if you're thinkin' about stayin' around these parts."

The lady looked at Momma2, and I think I saw her smile a little 'cuz her lips turned up at the edges. She tipped her head to the side and I could see a dimple, big as a nickel, plant itself on the side of her cheek. "Ma'am, I saved all my money to buy that car. I think she's a real beauty, don't you? She may not be practical, but she's dependable and I'm hoping to keep her if you let me."

"Hummm," Momma2 breathed out loud then she turned to Junie Bird. "Junie Bird, this here's Kate and that there lady in that fancy car over there is Essie Lou. They're gonna be stayin' over to the slave house for the summer. You're gonna be seein' 'em from time to time. Take your time gettin' to know 'em."

The driver lady looked over at Momma2, and her eyes got kinda wet for a minute. "Ma'am, are you saying we can stay?"

"I suppose I am," said Momma2. "I suppose I am. Now, don't be thinkin' the house you gonna be livin' in is fancy like your car, 'cuz it's not. It'll keep you warm and dry. I cleaned it out last week, so it's fit for livin'. You can fix it the way you like. It's only got one bed, so you and your sister have to sleep together. The kitchen's got all the fixin's for cookin', and there's an outhouse out back we can all use. I can get you food next time we go to town, but 'til then, you can eat with us. I'll take you over to the house then show you 'round the orchard. I s'pect Essie Lou to help me with Junie Bird and Tilly."

As she said my name, Momma2 looked over to me. "Tilly, get over here! You been standin' there mindin' all our business, so come over and make yourself known." I walked over to the lady and put out my hand like I knew what I was suppose to do.

"Tilly, huh? I like that name. Your Momma gave you a good one." She looked over to Momma2 like that was a compliment Momma2 was suppose to have.

"I'm not her momma. Junie Bird's her momma, but she calls me Momma2 'cuz she got confused when she was little when Junie Bird called me Momma. I'm her Momma, too, that's how it is."

"Well, Tilly, you've got a good name, and I like it. My name's Kate. It's nice to meet you." She shook my hand and smiled at me makin' that dimple show itself. "Come over and meet my sister."

I walked over to the car and looked at the lady inside. If Junie Bird was beautiful, this lady was a looker. Her blonde curly hair framed her face like a picture show woman. She had dark brown eyes and her skin was milky white. I could see she was a small framed lady 'cuz her dress seemed to billow around her like a tent. She was silent when I got to the car, but her eyes held mine with a look that made me think of Bossy when we had to pull her calf away from her milk.

"Essie Lou, this is Tilly. She's going to be part of our new life," Kate said it slowly and softly.

I never thought of myself as part of someone's new life, but I guess that was the truth of it. When someone new comes into what you know and they don't, then I guess we all get to add to our life in a way that might surprise us.

Essie Lou nodded her head and smiled at me, but her smile was weak. I took her hand when she held it out to me. I was surprised to find it was as small as mine.

Kate took her hand and said, "Essie, I'm going to talk with Mrs. Harris about our new job. I'd like you to come with me to meet her."

Kate seemed nervous to ask Essie Lou to come and meet Momma2, but bein' as she had had an accident, I was guessin' she wasn't quite finished with healin'.

As Essie Lou got out of the car, Kate took her elbow. "Come on, now, it's okay. She's not going to bite us."

All three of us went 'round that car and walked over to Momma2. She was standin' there watchin' ever'thing goin' on. When Kate got to Momma2 with Essie Lou, Kate did the introducin'.

"Mrs. Harris, I want you to meet my sister, Essie Lou. Essie Lou, meet Mrs. Harris."

Essie Lou held out her hand to Momma2. Momma2 took it and held it for longer than I thought was natural. Seemed like she was talkin' to Essie Lou through her hand.

"It's nice to meet you, Essie. I think you and my girl, Junie Bird, will get along just fine." She turned to me and spoke quiet like. " Tilly, Miss Essie Lou won't need any of your thousand questions. You hear me?"

I looked over to her like she was talkin' to someone else. "Well, 'course I do, Momma2, how's she suppose to answer questions if'n she's not talkin' to nobody?"

Momma2 nodded to me, then continued talkin' to Kate. "I'm gonna walk you down to the slave house. That's what we call it 'cuz some ol' slaves lived there way before we owned this place, and it still carries that name. It's not too far from here. It'll be a nice walk after drivin' in *that* car." The way she said *"that"* car made me know she still wasn't partial to it.

Kate and Essie Lou walked with Momma2 and I followed 'em. Junie Bird went back into the house. I could hear her hummin' as we left.

When it was springtime, the slave house looked like a house the seven dwarfs would have loved to live in. It was ol' an' tattered, but it was surrounded by those dogwood trees that was bloomin' with their beauty and fillin' the air with their sweet smell. The Eve tree was green and the ol' moss growin' up its trunk made it look like it was dressed to go to a ball. The early wildflowers was already out. They made it look like someone planned their appearance, even though no one did. They just did the job themselves.

Momma2 had cleaned the slave house out, and I could see the shine on the windows ready to be looked out of. Kate and Essie Lou slowed down as Momma2 got to the steps. "This here's the slave house. It's yours for your job time. The wood stacked out back is yours to use in your cook stove, and the pump to the side has good drinking water. There's a copper bath tank to the side of the house. Nobody can see y'all gettin' clean. Y'all have to heat the water before you get in, or you might not be so happy in it. Bed's made up and ready for sleepin'. I'm thinkin' you better keep that car parked up near our house 'cuz' there's no road down here. You just keep the keys in it 'case Zeke's got to move it for some good reason. You get your stuff unloaded then come back up to the house. We'll go meet Zeke and then have dinner. Got a pot of beans on with ham. Tilly, go out to the orchard and tell Zeke he's got a helper for the summer."

I left 'em there and took out runnin' for the orchard. It weren't often I had somethin' to tell Zeke he didn't know. This was my first time and I was makin' a beeline for him.

"Zeke, Zeke!" I yelled his name at the top of my lungs. "Zeke, I gotta tell ya somethin'!"

Zeke poked his head out from under a branch wipin' his head with a red hanky he had in his overalls. "What you yellin' 'bout chil'? Snake gottcha?"

I was pantin' and sweatin' when I stopped in front of him. "Zeke, you never gonna believe it, Momma2 done hired a woman to work on the farm."

For all my seven years, the only workers on the farm had been men. Mostly darkies when the fruit came on and sometimes drifters that needed a job for a short while. The Putter twins would be comin' on in a few weeks, but today was a miracle day 'cuz a woman was gonna be Zeke's firsthand worker.

Zeke looked at me for a second then bent down and grabbed his ol' jug of water and took a long, hard drink. He put it down on the ground, then wiped his head with his hanky again. No matter when, Zeke was always wet with work. "Tilly, you ain't tellin' ol' Zeke tales now are ya, girly?"

"No, Zeke, I'm tellin' you the truth as I know it. Momma2's gonna be bringin' a woman named Kate down to meet ya.. She's got a sister too. Her name's Essie Lou, but she don't talk any. She had some kinda accident made her words not work. She's a real pretty girl. Kinda little though; doesn't seem like she could do much work. But that Kate, she's a big'un. She looks like she could lift a wheelbarrow anytime she wanted."

Zeke thought a bit then took up his water again. After he finished his drink, he said, "Thanks for bringin' me the news, Tilly girl. I 'preciate it." He left me standin' there and went back to his work.

I walked back to the house, and when I got there, I saw Kate and Essie Lou pullin' stuff out of their car and walkin' it to the slave house. Kate did the heavy carrin'. Essie Lou piled clothes in her arms and walked behind Kate. It took 'em a good hour of goin' back and forth to get it all unloaded. They must a done some puttin' away too 'cuz they took some time gettin' back to the house. I heard 'em when they got to the door.

Junie Bird was sittin' in her rockin' chair just rockin' and hummin'. She didn't have any quiltin' goin' on; she was just in her head-place hummin' away.

Momma2 met 'em at the door and invited 'em in. "Come on in for a minute, girls. The bread is ready to take out and I need to get it out before I take off to the orchard with ya. Tilly, show 'em around so they know where ever'thing is."

I waited a minute 'cuz havin' new people in the house was like havin' company, and I didn't 'xactly know how to do company. I just started talkin' and pointin' at stuff, figurin' that was good enough."

When I got to the place where Grandpa Poe's books was kept, Momma2 called over for us to come on. We all followed her out to the orchard. Kate asked questions about the kinds of apples we grew and how many trees we had. She asked about our waterin' system and how we fertilized and asked if we kept bees. I listened for a while and thought she was kind of *a thousand questions kind of person* herself.

When Momma2 saw Zeke, she called out to him. He stopped what he was doin' and came up to all of us. Once again, he had his hanky out wipin' his head, but he bowed his head when he saw the ladies. Momma2 spoke up. "Zeke, this here lady is gonna be workin' in the orchard with ya. She comes from farmin' so she won't need schoolin' on what's she's suppose to do. If she don't get it after a week, you let me know. A week seems fair to see if she can do the work."

Momma2 wasn't really asking Zeke or Kate if that week was good enough. It was her bein' boss, and she was goin' by that.

Kate put out her hand to shake Zeke's, but he didn't take it. He bowed his head and said, "Yes, ma'am, Miss Lila. That be as it be. It's nice to meet ya, Miss Kate."

I saw Kate's hand go down, again, the second time it had reached for a hand and only got air. She seemed to understand and put her hand in her pant's pocket. Safe.

"Kate will begin work tomorrow, Zeke. She has her sister with her. They'll be stayin' at the slave house. They'll eat with us 'til we get 'em some groceries next trip to town. She'll be ready to go when you are."

"I'll work hard, Mr. Zeke," Kate said. " I won't be any trouble for you." She looked at Zeke when she was talkin', then she bowed her head, too. I figured I was gonna like anyone who called Zeke *"Mister"* and bowed her head to him like he did to her.

Chapter 6

When I woke up that mornin', the rain was running down my win'da like it was a curtain of water. I had heard it rainin' in the middle of the night and knew it was probably not gonna be a work outside kinda day. Those days didn't happen too often, so I was kinda lookin' forward to it. I had a book I really wanted to read.

Last week, when we went to Siloam Springs, Momma2 took me to the library for the first time and I got to pick out a book of my very own to read. When Momma2 parked outside the buildin', I stared at it not believin' I was really gonna go inta it. It was made from all brick. Our house, the barn, and near ever' store in Siloam Springs was made of wood. Just the important buildin's like the college and the library was made from bricks and that's what I was starin' at as I walked up the stairs.

Momma2 pulled the door open, 'cuz they was too big for my arms to pull back. When she opened the door I could hardly believe my eyes. They was books from the bottom of the floor to the top of the ceilin' and I mean ever'where. Some of the shelves had ladders runnin' up 'em, just so's people could find what they wanted. I took my first step inside and tried to take it all in. Momma2 nudged me with her elbow. "We don't have all day for book gettin', Tilly. Let's find where you need to look."

She took me by the arm and lead me over to the section that had books she thought I should pick from. I took a deep breath, lettin' all my air out at one time. I felt like a queen in her castle. Momma2 went off lookin' for some-thin' she liked and left me to find my own. There was 'bout a million choices.

I looked all around tryin' to find the best book for my first. I turned pages and read pieces, and then, when I found *Black Beauty*, I knew I found the perfect book for me. I carried that book to the librarian at the front of the library and handed it off to her to put my name in it like the other names I saw written down on its check out slip.

Momma2 had to sign her name on it, too, 'cuz they wasn't trustin' a seven year old to take any of their books out of the buildin'. I carried it out like it was precious gold with the biggest grin on my face I ever' had. Junie Bird was waitin' outside on the grass with Kate and Essie Lou. They was just sittin' there under a tree playin' with some string on their fingers waitin' for us to come out. Zeke was in the truck watchin' the supplies.

Essie Lou sat in the front of the truck between Momma2 an' Zeke 'cuz her body was so tiny it could squeeze in just right. Kate and Junie Bird and me piled in the back. When we got goin', I started to read my book, but it made my head kinda' dizzy. I didn't want any of that *favorite red egg business* comin' back to me, so I stopped and just held it in my lap.

Kate was sittin' by the tailgate of the truck facin' me and Junie Bird. We had our backs to the win'da of the truck, so we could see what was comin' up on us.

Kate had made it way past her week on the farm. She was a good worker. She was as wet and sweaty as Zeke ever' day, and she didn't moan one bit about workin' like a man. She knew farmin'. She dug in the dirt, fixed branches, spread fertilizer, not even pinchin' up her nose when she did, and she still called Zeke "Mister" which made me and Momma2 plenty happy. She didn't wear a hat like Momma2, so her skin was gettin' red and brown all at once. When she smiled, her white straight teeth stood out from that sun-brown skin like a flash of white underwear on Momma2's clothesline. She was pretty, too, but not like her sister. Kate was sittin' in the truck lookin' at the places on the side of the road and askin' me questions about who lived in each of the houses and what I knew about 'em. She liked to talk, and she liked to know.

The first week they was with us, Kate and Essie Lou ate with us ever' meal. Our table was a pine wood table with benches on each side, so it could hold eight people easy. Momma2 and Grandpa Poe had planned on a big family, but Junie Bird put a stop to that plan.

Kate and Essie Lou was quiet the first night, and even Kate didn't talk much. 'Course Essie Lou just watched kinda shy like and didn't say a word. Her quiet made Junie Bird's hummin' sound like a conversation. When someone's only quiet, you never know how their mind's a thinkin', and you don't get to guess on 'em like the ones that talk out loud.

Essie Lou sat right next to me on the bench, so I watched her out of the corner of my eye. She just put food in her mouth and chewed it up. Not much chewin' was needed on the bean part, but the ham needed a little. Her mouth worked just fine, but her words were broken. It was curious that a person could think about what ever'body else was sayin' and not open her mouth to say somethin' back.

Kate and Essie Lou both got up after dinner that first night and just started cleanin' up the dishes and the kitchen. Since that was my chore, I was right thankful for 'em. Momma2 didn't stop 'em from helpin'. I think she was curious to see how they joined in with what needed done. I could tell she liked their way.

After dinner, Kate thanked Momma2 for the meal, carryin' on 'bout how delicious it was. Ham and beans was one of my favorites, so I liked her carryin' on hopin' Momma2 would make it again soon. When they left the house the first night, Momma2 gave 'em an old kerosene lantern to take with 'em so they could find their way back to the slave house. I watched 'em as they left, Kate leadin' the way with the light and Essie Lou with her hand on Kate's shoulder followin' behind like she was a dog on a rope. I guess she was afraid to trip or somethin' cause she kept her head down as she walked.

When the sun come up the next mornin', Kate was at the door of the house, ready to work 'fore I had even pushed my blankets off me. I could hear her talkin' to Momma2 in the kitchen. I jumped to it and made my bed kinda hurried to make sure I didn't miss nothin' goin' on out there.

I could hear Momma2 talkin' "You bring Essie Lou in here to eat some breakfast before ya'll get started. Zeke'll be out on the tractor already and after you finish eatin', I'll walk you out to the orchard to get goin. I don't expect you to work on an empty stomach, so go on now and get your sister."

Kate left and came back a few minutes later with Essie Lou right behind her. Seemed like Essie Lou was the followin' kinda girl. Momma2 had her bread and jam and hard-boiled eggs out on the table. The sisters ate while Momma2 laid out the day.

Kate looked up from her plate when Momma2 said, "After breakfast, Kate, you and me will go down and get you started with Zeke. He'll be your boss in the orchard, and you are to be fair with him.

"Don't be givin' me eyes on that. You gotta know how most people think about darkies being their boss, but I'm not most people, and Zeke's your boss. You got that, girl?"

It really wasn't a question, but Kate answered it with a, "Yes ma'am, I do."

"Essie Lou, you gonna keep Junie Bird company during the day. She never had anybody keep her company, and I think that will be good for her. She don't talk much, so you don't need to worry about words. Just make sure she's doing okay. Your sister says you sew, so you can help her with her quiltin' if'n it's somethin' you want to do. You just watch over her. That's what I expect from you.

Essie Lou didn't say anythin'—she just looked at Momma2 and nodded. She looked like she was finished with eatin', so she picked up her plate and went to the kitchen to start cleanin'. Kate brought her dishes to the sink and left them for Essie Lou to clean. She patted Essie Lou real kind like on the back. Essie Lou looked at her and smiled. It was the first time I saw her smile, and it made her look even prettier than when she was just sittin' in the car. She had the kinda' look I'd seen on the movie house posters.

When Momma2 took off her apron and hung it up on the hook near the back porch, Kate followed her outside. I went with 'em 'cuz I was wonderin' how a woman would work with Zeke.

Zeke had been the boss of the orchard for all my years and years before me, too. He was really smart at doin' it. Momma2 said he could make apples grow on a dogwood, but I don't think he ever did that.

Zeke always ate dinner with us, but he made his own breakfast and lunch. Momma2 always sent food with him when he left after our dinner. He was always workin' before the sun was up in the mornin', and today was no exception. He was runnin' the tractor down the rows of trees workin' up the spring dirt. When he saw us comin', he turned off the engine, pulled his handkerchief from his pocket, and wiped his forehead. He was already wet with work.

He got down from the tractor and spoke his good mornin'.

"Mornin' ladies. Nice day for workin' outside ain't it? Just listen to them birds—they be singin' good mornin' to all of us."

Zeke always made out like the world was his personal friend, and ever'thing that breathed the air same, as him, was on his side of makin' the day a good one.

"Good morning, Mr. Zeke." Kate was first to say, and she put out her hand for him to shake. This time he took it and their eyes looked at each other. Zeke didn't hold his look for long, but Kate didn't wipe off his hand like I'd seen other people do when a darkie touched 'em for some reason.

Momma2 looked over at Zeke, then to Kate. "Kate, do what Zeke says." Then she turned and left 'em to work. I watched Momma2 walk back to the house, but I stayed to watch Kate look at Zeke.

"Mr. Zeke, my father was a farmer and I helped him. I know you'll know things a different way than what I learned, so you just tell me what to do and show me how you do it, so I don't get it wrong. I'll try hard to learn your way."

Zeke still had his handkerchief in his hand. He put it back in his pocket and turned to the tractor 'fore he started speakin'. "I needs yous to pick up all the dead branches I done cut and pile 'em at the end of each of the rows. When I's finished with the tractor work, then you and me's gonna put 'em in a big pile to burn this fall. They's a wheelbarra in the next row. Yous use that for the haulin'."

Kate didn't wait for Zeke to give her a second talkin'. She nodded her head with a "yessir." She ran to the next row and I saw her flyin' back with the wheelbarrow, makin' a beeline for the branches. I could tell, by the end of the day, she'd be wet with work, too.

I did my morn' chores then went back to the house to peak in on Essie Lou and Junie Bird. I had the shock of my life when I got there. Those two was sittin' by the quilt with needles goin' in and out, not sayin' a word, and Junie Bird was hummin' like she was in her happy place.

After all these years, I knew what Junie Bird's hummin' meant. If she hummed real loud and hard, then she was nervous or worried, but if she hummed real soft, then she was in her happy place. This mornin', Junie Bird was sewin' with Essie Lou, and she was in her happy place. Momma2 must of noticed it, too, 'cuz she walked up behind Essie Lou and said, "Looks to me like your hands know what to do with a needle." She patted her on the back, and Essie Lou startled at Momma2's touch.

Momma2 backed away a little, but smiled at her as she left. Momma2 wasn't known much for smilin', so I knew she was in her happy place, too.

That's how the days went, week by week. Kate and Essie Lou ate with us the first week, 'cuz of 'em not havin' food at the slave house, but when we went to town that first weekend, they got food for themselves. They cooked dinner for themselves, but they still came to the house for breakfast, and Momma2 had Essie Lou make Kate's lunch for her to take to the orchard. Essie Lou stayed at the house with Junie Bird 'til Kate came and got her after work; then the two of 'em would go back to the slave house. I guess they fixed their dinner, then went to bed. Kate looked like she was wore out ever' night, but she never complained, and she was always happy to see Essie Lou when she finished her workin'.

I sometimes wished I had a sister to like like they like each other. All I had was Junie Bird and she wasn't much for likin'.

When the rainy day kept us in, I heard Junie Bird do her loud hummin' when she got up. If'n she did that all day, I knew I wasn't gonna get my readin' done 'cuz my mind wouldn't be wantin' to think about the story—it would be wantin' to shut her up. Momma2 was in the room talkin' real quiet to her. "It's gonna be ok, Junie Bird. The rain's a good thing. Gonna water the apples for us and we's gonna get lots of apples to sell in the fall. You don't worry none about this rain noise, child. It's a bath for the earth."

Momma2 kept talkin' to Junie Bird for a long time, and pretty soon, she was quiet and lost in her mind someplace. I grabbed my library book, sat by the wood stove, and opened it and read.

Books were a wonder to me. When I first learned to read I imagined all the letters in the ABC's marching on the pages wanting me to know what they was sayin'. I read all of Grandpa Poe's science books and ever'thing that came into the house. This library book was the first book I ever read that I chose just for me. Black Beauty was speakin' to me in horse language while I read that book. I could pretend sometimes I wasn't just in this house with Junie Bird and Momma2, but I was in a pasture in a English countryside with a bunch of my friend horses, just passin' the day. 'Course, when the book told the horrible things people did ta horses, it could make me flamin' mad, and I wanted to cry out with that madness. But I kept that madness in me, I didn't want to be actin' like Junie Bird.

I was so absorbed in the story, I didn't hear the poundin' on the door at first. When I finally heard it, I ran to see who it was. It was Kate. She was wet with rain and looked pretty bad worried. She asked Momma2 to come down to the slave house to see Essie Lou. Essie Lou was sick, and Kate didn't know what to do.

Momma2 put on her slicker—that's what she called her coat that was heavy with some kinda rubber coatin'. She put it on over her head and took off down the path with Kate. It was a good long time 'for she got back, and when she did, she had worry on her face, too. She didn't say anything. I was afraid to ask what was wrong with Essie Lou, scared she'd be too sick to take care of Junie Bird—then I'd have to do it.

Momma2 just went back to makin' bread. I put down my book and went over to see if I could help her. Sometimes she'd let me punch down the dough for her. I was hopin' this was one of those days.

When I got to the kitchen, I could see Momma2's head shakin' back and forth like she was talkin' to herself and answerin' herself. Whatever the question was, she was shakin' her head *'no'* real hard, makin' sure her brain heard it.

"Momma2, what ya thinkin' is wrong with Essie Lou? She needin' Doc Gibbs?" Momma2 musta been real deep in her thoughts, 'cuz she jumped when she heard me talk.

"Tilly, don't be sneakin' up on people like that! You want to scare life out of 'em, girl?"

I didn't usually scare Momma2, so it made me scared that I scared her. I guess she could tell that and she signaled me over to the bread makin' bowl. "Wash up your hands and help me with this bread, will ya? I'm not sure I have enough punch in me today to work it good."

She never did answer my question.

I ran my hands under the water that sat in the sink ready for any washin' needin' done, then wiped 'em on the tea towel hangin' on the hook under the sink. Like her aprons, the tea towels was all made from the floor sacks that Momma2 bought and this one was pretty worn out. Momma2 wouldn't throw nothin' out 'til it was rags for cleanin'. This tea towel was still in the *use it* place.

I pushed a kitchen chair over to the bread bowl on the ol' cuttin' table Momma2 used to cut ever'thing on. It set in the center of the kitchen, near the sink. When I got all settled, I waited for Momma2 to give me the go ahead 'fore I stuck my hands in the dough and pushed down to knead it. Once she gave me the okay, I pushed with all my might makin' sure I got to the bottom of the bowl when I went down. It always looked a lot easier than it was. Momma2 punched her side and let me punch mine. Then she'd turn the bowl 'round and let me punch her side and she'd punch mine. Ever'thing was quiet. Junie Bird was in the livin' room rockin' in her chair not sayin' a word and Momma2 and me was in the kitchen not sayin' a word. It was rainin' hard outside. We listened to it beat down on the roof, wettin' the outside while we kept warm. I knew Momma2 had a worry about Essie Lou, but she weren't gonna be tellin' me what it was, so I just kept punchin' the bread dough and started thinkin' 'bout Black Beauty and his new master. Black Beauty sure didn't know what would be happenin' to him next, and I guess I didn't neither.

Chapter 7

Momma2 always says the rain brings the rats out, and it must be true 'cuz when the rain finally stopped two days later, the Putter boys showed up at our door lookin' to get hired again for the summer.

They was pretty much rat lookin' themselves, only one was fatter than the other. They was twins, but they looked like two different kinda rats. Remy was skinny and small lookin'. His hair was dirty blonde and, when I tell ya dirty, I'm meanin' that word. His hair looked like it never saw soap. In fact, when you looked at the back of his hair, his neck was dirty and seemed to have some sorta cursty stuff on it. I s'pose cleanin' wasn't high on their list for 'em ta do. Remy had a scar over his left eye that was deep and ugly. It made his eye look bigger than normal. I always hated lookin' at him and seein' that eye look back at me. Made me want to fix it with somethin'. Both twins had sharp noses and crooked teeth, and even though Remy had all his teeth, they was yella and they was dirty lookin', too.

Ronnie was a head taller than Remy and had man sized arms even though he was only 15 years old. His hair was brown with a tinge of red in it; not like Momma2's red, his red looked like he was leakin' red oil. It was chopped up, not cut even, and the cuttin' seemed to be missin' some spots. It was his missin' eye tooth that made him look like some pirate from a ship somewhere. Momma2 said the twins had a hard daddy, so their scars and missin' teeth may have had somethin' to do with their daddy but I didn't know that for sure. Like I said, they was rat lookin, and they was always sneakin' 'round like you needed to watch what they was doin'.

When Momma2 answered the door that mornin', I could see the boys in the door frame with their ol' raggy overalls hangin' off 'em. They was tryin' real hard to talk nice to Momma2 when she opened the door to 'em.

"Mornin', Miss Lila. We be out of school for the summer, and we's wonderin' if'n we could work for ya this summer 'til fall pickin' time comes on. We's ready to start tomarry if'n that's okay with'n y'all."

Remy did all the talkin'. Ronnie stood behind him with his rotten ol' hat in his hands and his head hung down like he was waitin' for a slap. Momma2 invited the twins in the house 'cuz that was how she was, always bein' polite an' all.

The boys come in, and when they did, they saw Junie Bird and Essie Lou by the quiltin' frame sewin' together. Essie Lou did not look up, and of course, ol' Junie Bird, half the time, didn't know what was goin' on, so she just kept in her own head about what she was doin'.

I could see the twins starring at Essie Lou and Momma2 did too. "Boys it isn't polite to stare at a person. That there is Essie Lou. She and her sister, Kate, are livin' down at the slave house this summer. Essie Lou is helpin' me with Junie Bird and Kate is helpin' Zeke in the orchard. You'll be workin' with her and Zeke both. Essie Lou don't talk, so don't be askin' her any questions."

As usual, Momma2 had her hands in her apron. She took them out and wiped 'em like they was wet when I knew well enough they wasn't. She watched the twins turn their heads to look at Essie Lou one more time, then they looked back at Momma2.

"You two be here tomorrow mornin' and get started. You know I pay once a month and I'll pay ya the same as last summer. If'n there's a good crop of apples and we get a fair sellin' price, I'll give you each a bonus pay in September for the extra we get paid. If'n the crop is short or we get stormed out, then you get what I get and that's how it is."

The boys looked up at her and nodded their heads. I couldn't tell if they'd been listenin' to her or not 'cuz the most I saw 'em do is keep tryin' *not* to look at Essie Lou.

When they left the house, Essie Lou lifted her head and looked at the door like she was glad they was gone. Like I said, it's hard to know what someone's thinkin' when they don't use their words for sayin' their thoughts.

After that rainy day when Kate came up to the house to get Momma2 to go down and see Essie Lou, I could see Momma2 watchin' Essie Lou real close like. She'd always talked real soft to Essie Lou and ask if she needed to lay down and rest, but Essie Lou never did. Her face was pale, and I thought her skin was lookin' a lot like onion paper. But she had a rosy colorin' in it that made her look clean and shiny.

Essie Lou was what Momma2 called a patient woman—one who could sit and listen to Junie Bird hum all day and not go screamin' out of the house. 'Course Essie Lou didn't scream none. She just nodded. And she always nodded 'yes'. Made me wonder what would make her head shake 'no'.

When the twins showed up for work the next day, they knocked at the door and stood there waitin' for Momma2 to invite 'em in. She didn't. "Boys, wait there and I'll be out to take you to Zeke."

I could see from their faces they was disappointed they didn't get to come in and take another peek at Essie Lou. That's what I was thinkin' anyway.

Momma2 headed out to the orchard with the twins taggin' behind her. I stayed in and started on the slop buckets. I was gettin' real good at doin' that chore without puttin' my nose in my sleeve. I walked outside carrin' the bucket and started out to the pigs. On my way, I could hear the tractor in the orchard and could imagine Zeke ridin' along singin' his ol' darkie songs as he drove.

Kate and Zeke had become a good workin' team. It was the end of May and she'd worked with him for four weeks now. One day, I heard Zeke tell Momma2, "That girl takes to farmin' like a cat takes to mice." That was high praise comin' from Zeke.

When Grandpa Poe died, Zeke stayed on with Momma2. Both of 'em lost the people they loved the most and they needed each other. If'n Momma2 and Zeke had other friends, no one knew it. They was friends for each other. Zeke was the one who kept the orchard goin', and Momma2 kept Zeke goin'. It worked for both of 'em. Junie Bird and me was the extras who needed lookin' after, and they both took care of lookin' after us.

After I finished with the pigs, I took to the trail goin' down to the creek. I hadn't been down there since my egg sickness, and I figured it was time to do some fishin'. Zeke had left my fishin' stuff down by the rock. I found it near my climbin' up place, when I got there. I didn't have no worms, but I took a stick, dug around a bit, and found a couple to get started with. I jumped up on the rock, threw my line in the water, and settled myself down waitin' for some fish ta come along and bite.

By noon, I'd caught a couple crappies, but they was too small to keep, so I threw 'em back to grow some more. Zeke taught me that when he taught me to fish. "No use eatin' the little ones, Tilly girl," he'd say. "They's got to gets big 'nuf ta make us some more fish for'n ya take 'em home ta cook."

Since I never had a daddy of my own, I guess Zeke was mine to claim. Whatever Momma2 didn't teach me, he did. I didn't attend public school. The school bus passed by our way ever' day durin' the school year. It picked up the Putter twins, but it didn't pick up me. Momma2 said I wasn't gonna go to school til she was good and ready to send me. She had taught me to read, and she and Zeke made sure I knew my numbers and how to figure all the store bills we got. I could tally up all the apple bins and could make marks on the apple sheets to see how much they weighed and how much they'd sell for when we brought 'em to market. I could weigh out anything on the big scale or the little one, and I could make change from any money people gave me, so I wasn't lackin' any learnin' far as Momma2 could see. She figured after I turned eight I would be big enough to take up for myself if 'n I needed to, and then she'd think 'bout sendin' me off. 'Til then, I got to learn everything there was to learn stayin' right here on the orchard. And it was a good class-room. I wasn't wantin' on goin' anywhere else!

I knew there was kids my age other places near us, but I never did play with any of 'em. Didn't have need 'cuz my mind played all by itself.

Today, when I was down at the creek after I finished up fishin', I put my pole away near the rock, then I spent some time throwin' rocks as far as my arm could throw. I loved to watch 'em land with a splash. The rocks made holes in the water when they landed, and the water shouted "hallaluah" with its splash. When I tired of that, I knelt down by the side of the creek and I gathered a bunch of little rocks and big rocks, then I made circles of rocks for the water to fill in and make little pools. I could spend a whole damn day just playin' in the water like that.

I use to love to make hidey holes under the rocks near the creek. I'd crawl in them and play like I was hidin' from some outlaw comin' to find me, but Momma2 put a stop to that when she came down lookin' for me one day. "Tilly, you be wantin' to invite some copperhead or water mocassins down there to play with ya?"

I hadn't thought of that before, but after she said that, it gave me the shivers just thinkin' 'bout it. I wasn't too fond of snakes.

When I finished playin' 'round the creek, I headed up to the house by the back way. The back way didn't have no trail, so I had to find the way through the trees and the bushes. The bushes was all grown out with leaves this time of year, so it made the goin' a little harder. I liked goin' that way' cuz it was always an adventure. I knew the way by heart and could find it blindfolded, but I liked to pretend it was a secret passage. That made it more interestin'.

Before I got to the house, I passed by the cemetery where Grandpa Poe and Belva and Zeke's baby girl was buried. I decided to stop in for a visit like Momma2 and Zeke did.

There was a fence 'round the cemetery protectin' it from animals, so I opened the gate real careful like and walked over to Zeke's baby girl's head-stone. I looked down on it for a while and just thought 'bout what it would be like to be covered with dirt for all the time you was suppose ta live. Zeke didn't get a chance to even hear her voice, and that made me sad for him. Zeke woulda been a real good daddy if'n his little girl coulda lived to see the light a day, but that didn't happen. I wondered what his little girl woulda looked like. Maybe she woulda been friends with Junie Bird, and they woulda played together, then Junie Bird wouldn'ta had to go to church to meet new people, but then I wouldn'ta been here, so I stopped thinkin' bout that.

When we was all together at dinner or driving ta town, Zeke talked about Belva, so I felt I knew her like a real live person. She was small and fun lovin'. Her hair was nappy and short, and her smile was big and broad. I could see the dancin' eyes Zeke talked 'bout ever' time I thought of her. *She was just too small to push a baby into the world.* That's what Zeke had told me.

I said my hellos and goodbyes to Zeke's family, then I went and sat on the bench by Grandpa Poe's grave. His headstone was tall, with the words: "Poe, 1900–1945." It also had a heart on it with room for another name when the time come for Momma2 to join him in the ground.

Like I done told ya, I could add numbers and knew Grandpa Poe was 45 when he died. I knew he had been dead since right before I started breathin' the earth's air, so he had been in the ground 7 years. I seen pictures of him and knew his look. He was taller than Momma2 by a good head. The picture by her bed was one of the two of 'em standin' together by the ol' truck—him with his hand on her shoulder and Momma2 with her head on his. They was both smilin', and I'm thinkin' Zeke musta took the picture. She also had a picture in the bedroom taken the day they was married, but the picture by the truck was the one she favored. She had a picture of Grandpa Poe when he was a little boy hangin' on the livin' room wall. His momma must a been right proud of him 'cuz the picture was in a special gold-lookin' oval frame with paintin' done on the picture to make him look like a prince. He looked a lot like Junie Bird. Had her eyes and face shape. Momma2 said he was the handsomest man she ever did see.

I didn't know how to talk to Grandpa Poe at the grave like Momma2 'cuz I didn't know him like her, but I figured since he was my grandpa, he'd know me talkin', so I just started on like he was there.

"Hey, Grandpa Poe, it's me, Tilly. I'm Junie Bird's girl, your granddaughter. I'm sorry I didn't get to know you like real people, but guess this 'ill do for what we have. I played a bit this mornin' down by the creek. I like the place you picked for the house here; gives me runnin' room, and the apples are doin' real good where ya planted 'em. Zeke's got himself a girl worker. That's a new one for ya. I bet ya never heard of a girl comin' to work on the orchard like that. Her name's Kate 'case ya want to know her. Her sister's named, Essie Lou. Essie Lou had a terrible accident and she don't talk. Can't imagine the accident that made her mouth not work except to smile. They's real nice girls, and Essie Lou keeps your girl happy sewin' and makin' string games all the time. The Putter twins is here for the summer. You never met 'em neither, 'lessin' you knew 'em when they was young'uns, but I s'pose you'd be like Momma2 and be sorry for 'em and give' em' a job. They are too dirty and sneaky for me ta like and they call Zeke "boy." I think you'd give 'em a thrashin' if'n you ever heard 'em do that. That's what I want ta do to 'em, but I let Momma2 take care of it when she hears 'em. Well, I guess I filled ya in on me for a while. Now I can see why Momma2 likes visitin' ya. You're right nice ta talk to. I'll come back another time. Be seein' ya, Grandpa Poe."

I stood there for a bit lettin' my words sink down into the earth for him to hear, then I started back up to the house. The tractor was busy in the orchard, and I knew Kate and the Putter twins was busy with their work. I wondered how the Putter boys liked workin' with Kate.

When I got near the outhouse, I heard a sound I recognized from when I was sick with my Easter egg. Someone was pukin' to beat the band and I could hear 'em moan like they was dyin'.

"You okay in there?" I asked concerned like 'cuz I knew I might need to run get Momma2, but nobody answered me. They just kept pukin' their guts out. I was 'bout ready to run get Momma2 when I heard the door creak open. It was Essie Lou. She was wipin' her mouth with the back of her hand as she stepped out the door.

"Essie Lou, you okay?" I asked. "You need your sister or Momma 2?"

Essie Lou looked at me with scared eyes and shook her head no. It was like her head was screamin' that word to me. I just looked back at her. I could hear what her head shakin' was sayin'.

"Okay," I said real quiet like 'cuz I knew her head shake meant that was the end of the askin'.

She wiped at her mouth again then reached for my hand. As I held out my hand, she looked down at me and patted my hand real soft like. She led me back to the house in silence.

Chapter 8

When Momma2 come in the house through the back porch, I knew we had one less chicken to pick eggs outa. She had washed her hands under the pump water to get the blood offa her, but there was still bits a feathers around her, and her eyes had water in 'em like she'd been cryin'. I knew she was headin' for the sink. She needed soap to get clean the way she wanted to be, and she didn't want nobody askin' her what she done. She wasn't fonda killin' anything, but food was food and, when the chickens got old and stopped layin', they was food. We was gonna have fried chicken for Sunday dinner and I could hardly wait!

When she was finished cleanin' up her hands, she pulled the big wash basin out from under the sink and took the butcherin' knife out of the carvin' box. She put on her ol' apron and headed out the door. She didn't tell me where she was goin' 'cuz I knew well 'nuf.

Essie Lou was plaiting Junie Bird's hair, and they was listenin' to the radio music. Momma2 didn't turn the radio on on account it cost electricity to run it, but when Essie Lou pointed to it the other day, Momma2 turned it on for her to listen. Her and Junie Bird just sat by the radio like two beautiful princesses listenin' to music fill the house like it was Christmas or somethin'. I liked stories on the radio but wasn't particular about music noise, so I headed outside with Momma2.

I followed her to the place next to the henhouse that had an ol' stump of a tree. Momma2 used that stump to lay the chickens on to chop off their heads. That had already been done and the dead chicken was hangin' on the clothesline by its feet dripping all its blood out. It still had feathers on it. The feather pickin' part, was the hardest part and it stunk to high heavens when she was pluckin' 'em in the hot water. Momma2 had started a fire in the fire pit out back. After she filled the big pot that was hangin' on the back of the house full of water from the pump, she set it on the fire pit and let it steam up and get ta boilin'. When it had boiled up good and hot, she took that chicken off the line and swished it 'round and 'round in that boilin' water. That got the feathers started for pluckin' and that got the stink started, too.

When she finished that, she took the chicken over ta the stump and started pluckin' feathers out. She put the feathers on a sheet on the ground to save for Junie Bird to fill her quilts when they was dry. Momma2 saved ever'thing and chicken feathers was no exception. After she got the chicken plucked of all its feathers, she cleaned the bird out, then hung it back up on the clothesline to dry out. It would be ready to butcher later on. I just watched and didn't get in her way. Butcherin' animals was Momma2's quiet time, and she didn't want any talkin' goin' on whilst she was doin' it.

I watched her clean her hands off, then take her apron off and wipe her hands dry. When she went back inside the house, she carried the butcher knife and apron and put them both where they belonged—the knife back in the box and the apron 'side the ol' washin' machine where she'd wash it with the rest of the dirty clothes on Monday.

Momma2 had a system for livin' and she kept to that system without fail. She didn't like nobody messin' with her days to do things. Monday she washed clothes. She put ever'thing out on the line to dry, and if there was any ironin' to get done, that was a Tuesday job. Wednesday she made bread, and Thursday she put sheets on the line to air out. She didn't always wash sheets 'ever week 'cuz she said they just needed the air to clean 'em up. Friday she worked in the garden gettin' at the weeds, and Saturday was the day we all went ta town to get supplies. Today was Sunday, the day we had dinner in the middle of the day, then took it easy.

Sometimes on Sunday Zeke would bring over his handmade zither, and we'd all sit 'round the fire pit and sing ol' darkie songs with him. Sometimes we'd sing some songs Momma2 knew, but she didn't know many. *Row, Row, Row Your Boat* was one of 'em Momma2 knew and we had fun takin' turns startin' the song at different times. It made the song sound like it was followin' itself.

Now that we had Kate and Essie Lou here, they joined in for our together time. Essie Lou didn't sing, of course, but she clapped to the music like she knew the words. Junie Bird just rocked in her chair lettin' the time go by.

One Sunday, Kate sang us a song she knew and it was a good one. It was *Good Night Irene, Goodnight* and we all tried to learn it so's we could sing along with her. When she sang it, she looked at Essie Lou and Essie Lou looked at her. They was sure sweet feelin' sisters; I could tell.

The day the chicken come to dinner, I ran down to the slave house to tell Kate and Essie Lou what we was havin'. Zeke didn't need ta know 'cuz he was there ever' Sunday and knew sometimes a fried chicken was our meal. It was a big day for me 'cuz next to beans and ham, nothin' compared to fried chicken. Now that Momma2 had the chicken butchered it was soakin' in buttermilk. Pretty soon she'd have it in the big iron skillet fryin' in a lot of bacon grease. I helped her cut up potatoes. On Friday, Momma2 had picked peas from the garden. She had Junie Bird and Essie Lou shell 'em, so we was gonna have a right fine dinner, and I was ever so happy Kate and Essie Lou was gonna be there to eat with us.

When I got to the slave house, I could hear Kate talkin' to Essie Lou. Her voice was quiet. It sounded like she was whisperin', but she wasn't. I could hear her words from outside. I wasn't even sneakin' up to hear Kate's words.

"Don't worry, sweetheart." I heard Kate say. "It'll be alright. I'm right here, and I'm not going anywhere. Don't worry, now."

I didn't know how Kate could know Essie Lou was worried on a count a' Essie Lou didn't talk to tell her, but it sounded like Kate knew her from the inside, and I was guessin' it was 'cuz they was good sisters. I knocked on their door and Kate answered. "Well, well, Miss Tilly, how are you, today?" She talked ta me like there was no worry in the room behind her, but I could see Essie Lou had tears in her eyes.

Essie Lou had been sick a lot. Seemed like ever' mornin' I seen her headin' for the outhouse to empty her breakfast. I tattled on her ta Momma2, but Momma2 just said, "Tilly, Essy Lou's gonna be fine, just a little sickness 'cuz of her accident. Nothin' for you to worry about. Just go on with your business and let her be sick by herself."

That was kinda hard ta do 'cuz listenin' to someone puke wasn't 'xactly what I liked to hear—made me think too hard on my own pukin' time and that was not somethin' good ta think on.

I did let her be, and Junie Bird didn't seem to notice none. Toward the middle of June, I saw Essie Lou stop her mornin' sick, so I thought maybe her accident time was gonna get better, but she still didn't use her words.

It had been a good springtime havin' Kate and Essie Lou at the orchard. Zeke and Kate worked like crazy. We had good rains off and on to water the apples. The winds and cold wasn't bad enough to freeze anythin' off the trees. When the sweet smellin' blossoms was out in full, the orchards looked like it was a ballroom ready for the king and queen of England to come down the rows in a carriage pulled by prancin' horses. I loved runnin' through the trees when the blossoms started to fall off. I let 'em rain down on me like snow. Since it didn't snow much in Arkansas, it was a good pretend time for me.

The blossoms was already down on the ground now, and little tiny apples was poppin' out of that startin' place each blossom made. Seemed like Mother Nature sure had surprisin' ways to do things—makin' a tree start an apple like it was a present all wrapped up in a blossom. Who coulda figured that one out 'cept the One who made it all happen?

I never could figure out who 'actly did make all the things on earth, 'cludin' me. Seemed like some magical hands had to have done it 'cuz it sure beat anything I could think of. Like big pigs, made little pigs and big cows made little cows, and then bam! Apples come from tree blossoms. That's some magic all right.

There was no magic goin' on with Kate and Essie Lou. Essie Lou was lookin' more an' more worried and Kate was pretendin' she wasn't, but I could see it plain as day. Essie Lou had worry spread over her face like a storm brewin'. I looked at Kate real si'pcious like. My eyes tried not to narrow down, but I could feel 'em doin' that when I told 'em 'bout comin' to the house for chicken dinner. I told 'em we'd be havin' the peas we shelled yesterday, hopin' that would make Essie Lou smile. She tried to make her mouth give in to a smilin' look, but I could tell it was hard work for her. I told 'em we'd be eatin' in 'bout an hour, and then Zeke was gonna bring his zither over for some singin'. When I asked him to do that earlier he'd said, "Tilly, nothin' makes the week end better than some singin'."

I ran back over to the house and took a long cold drink from the pump 'fore I went back inside. The house smelled so good I could eat the air in it. How did those smells float around in the air like that? There was no end to the magic the earth had.

When I heard Kate and Essie Lou come up the back steps, I hurried to open the door for 'em. They was gettin' to be right at home at our house and I was likin' havin' 'em with us; kept it interestin' havin' new people at our table, and Kate made good talk.

Momma2 wasn't too nosy 'bout where they come from, but I asked Kate questions 'bout her farm. She didn't get real 'pecific, but said her farm was in a little town called Hudson, New York. That's why she talked like a Yankee. New York was as Yankee as you could get. She said Zeke did things different than her daddy, but Zeke's ways were real good. Zeke didn't say anything when she said that, but I could guess that made him feel right proud.

One Saturday, when we was in town gettin' supplies, Zeke bought a red handkerchief, like the one he carries in his pocket. When we got back to the house, he handed it to Kate and said, "You's be sweatin', chil. You's might be needin' this." Then he turned 'round and went back to the barn. I could see Kate's eyes get water in' em, but she never said nothing 'cuz Zeke was gone 'fore she could get any words out. After that, I seen Kate with that red hand-kerchief tied 'round her head like she was an ol' mammy darkie. She looked real cute that way. I could see Zeke liked how she wore it, but I'm bettin' he never said such.

After we finished our chicken dinner and cleaned up the dishes and the kitchen, we all went outside in the backyard. Zeke got some wood from the pile out back of the house and started a small fire in the pit. Years before he had built little seat benches around the pit, so's we could sit and sing. We all took a seat, and he got his zither out and started singin'.

Junie Bird started playin' with her braid and hummin' to music in her own head. We always had to ignore her doin' that 'cuz her hummin' never went 'long with any sound we was listenin' to. She was her own band.

I loved ol' Zeke's voice. It was rough and soft at the same time. He could make sounds that made ya feel like your heart wanted to dance and sometimes his songs would be so lonely soundin', it almost made me want to cry, but I never did.

When he finished his last song, Kate asked Momma2 to tell a story 'bout Grandpa Poe.

Momma2 looked over at her and smiled. "Well now, why y'all want to hear 'bout somebody you never gonna meet?"

Kate looked at Momma2. "Miss Lila, I hear you say his name a lot. I was just curious about him. What he was like and all. But I don't want you to be telling anything you don't want to tell."

Momma2 put down her head for a minute then lifted it and stared at the fire burnin' in the pit. "Poe was a man who couldn't lie. Once, when I was carryin' Junie Bird, I asked him if I was too big to love. He looked over at me and said, "Not too big to love, Lila, but my arms aint' gettin' 'round y'all like they use ta."

Momma2 looked up at Kate and smiled like she was rememberin' all over again. Then she said, "His answer made me laugh so hard I cried real tears. He was a good man and lots of fun."

Momma2 didn't have to finish that sentence with *she missed him* 'cuz those words were stuck in the air all silent like.

Kate smiled and so did Zeke. Essie Lou looked at Momma2 with a deepness I couldn't understand, but I knew she was thinkin' somethin' that I wish her words would say.

When the fire started goin' out, I asked Momma2 if'n I could sleep on the porch roof. I'd started doin' that when I was 6 years old. I wanted to sleep under the stars, and Momma2 didn't want me sleepin' on the ground and invitin' a snake to sleep with me. She was always worrin' me 'bout them wiggly things.

Anyway, our back porch roof was kinda flat and low hangin'. She piled old thick quilts up there and let me sleep under the stars all by myself. It was a warm night, and the stars were gonna be out full, so it would be a good night for star watchin'.

Momma2 nodded her head and asked Kate if'n she wanted to help her get quilts to get my bed ready for me. Kate went inside the house with Momma2 but Essie Lou stayed out with me and Junie Bird. Zeke said his good nights to all of us, picked up his zither, and left. I watched him go. His back was bendin' more than it use to, but he still held his head high and kept his steps with purpose.

When Momma2 and Kate came back, they had the quilts in their hands. I could tell Momma2 liked Kate's help. Momma2 put up the ladder by the side of the house and climbed up with the first load of quilts. Kate handed her the second load, and when Momma2 was finished with those she climbed down. "Tilly, you are *The Princess and the Pea*. I hope you have a good night's sleep."

I said good night to Kate and Essie Lou, then ran inside to get my pajamas on. My pajamas was old shirts Momma2 had outworn, but was good 'nuf for sleepin'. I loved my ol' pajamas 'cuz they was so soft.

I started to run out and climb up on the roof. "Don't you be goin' out without sayin' a good night, Girl." Momma2 put out her arms for me to climb into. I ran over to her and let her squeeze me goodnight. "Good night Momma2. I'm hopin' you sleep good, too."

I felt her squeeze me an extra time, then I looked at her when she was finished. I could see her love even though she didn't say the words.

She walked me outside and watched me climb the ladder to the roof and tuck myself in. She climbed up behind me to make sure I was covered. "If'n you get cold or scared, you climb on down and come inside, you hear me?"

"Yes, Momma2, I will," I answered, but I knew I wouldn't be cold 'cuz there was ten pounds a blankets for me to cover with, and I knew I wouldn't be scared 'cuz this was my home and nothin' scared me here. But I answered with what she needed to hear.

I could hear her go inside and talk to Junie Bird like Junie Bird would understand her. I knew she didn't and so did Momma2.

I watched the stars for a long time. I could name a lot of the constellations 'cuz Zeke and Momma2 had taught 'em to me on the nights we was all outside together. Some of the constellations had stories to 'em, and I could retell 'em like I was the grownup.

The Pleiades was my favorite constellation 'cuz it was seven sisters and I was always wantin' sisters of my own, but I couldn't see them in June 'cuz they come out when it was apple pickin' time. I stared up at the night sky and named all the constellations I knew and somewhere in the middle of namin' 'em, I fell asleep.

I don't know why I woke up, but I did. I was confused and thought I was in my bed. I looked around to look for my walls and winda. When I felt the brush of cool air walk across my face, I 'membered I was sleepin' on the porch roof and raised my head to listen to the sounds that woke me up.

At first, I wasn't sure if'n it'd been a dreamin' noise, but after I listened a minute I knew I weren't dreamin'. I heard somethin' for sure. I sat up real quiet like and looked in the darkness to see if'n I could see what I heard. The rustle was comin' from down by the slave house and it sounded like people creepin' through the bushes. I could hear the breathin' of someone. It was a sound that reminded me of an animal breathin' hard but tryin' not to be heard. Pretty soon the creepin' sound was comin' by the cemetery and goin' past it. They was heavy steps and light steps makin' their way through all that tangle of bushes.

I heard someone trip, and another person said somethin' that I couldn't make out, but they was words for sure and they didn't want no one to hear 'em talkin'. Pretty soon, the creepin' seemed far away, and then, it disappeared from my ears. It didn't disappear from my mind though. I wasn't 'xactly scared, but I wasn't none too comfortable neither. No one round our parts did any night time walkin' 'cuz you couldn't see a damn thing in the dark, and you could easy fall and kill yourself, so whoever was creepin' down behind the slave house and our house wasn't doing it 'so's we'd know they was there. They was creepin' in the dark, so's not to be seen. But I heard 'em. I heard 'em for sure, and I knew I better not tattle tell tomarra mornin' to Momma2 'cuz that might mean she wouldn't let me sleep outside again and I sure didn't want that ta happen.

Chapter 9

The apple press was pushed back against the wall in the barn. It wouldn't be comin' out until apples started fallin' in September, and it was only the end of June. I looked inside the ol' wooden apple barrel and sniffed. The ripe smell of apples was still left in there, and I couldn't wait for the time to come to press the ol' fallen apples that was no good for sellin', and make cider out of 'em. It was a time worth waitin' for.

The barn always smelled of apples and Zeke. Zeke's place was a lean-to, attached to the side of the barn next to the orchard, that Zeke built when Belva went in the ground with their baby. At that time, Grandpa Poe was livin' in the slave house, and Zeke thought a place by the barn and the orchard seemed the right place for him. The cemetery was right out back of the barn, too, so Zeke was close to his family. He fixed up the lean-to for his own. The wood was the same as the barn and had a color to it that seemed to go from inside to outside. When Momma2 came along, she made some curtains for his windas and a cover for the bottom of his cupboard. The colors added a warm feelin' to the room. Zeke's lean-to was really just one big room that was filled with his livin' needs. When you walked in the door, you could see the bed on the back wall piled high with quilts. Some of 'em was the ones Junie Bird had made for him, and some of 'em was ones his wife, Belva, had sewed when she was breathin' air. His bed always looked like you could just sink down in it and never find yourself and no one could ever find you.

Zeke's cookin' area was fixed up like a regular kitchen. It had a small cook stove and a table and a couple chairs. I s'pose Grandpa Poe use to visit him when he was a livin' man. But now, I did. I could sit on the chair and talk to Zeke while he cooked hisself some food. He didn't work out in the orchard on Sundays and, sometimes, I'd ask Momma2 if I could go have breakfast with Zeke. She always said "yes" to that ask.

That's where I was this Sunday. I was sitting on ol' Zeke's chair waitin' for him to cook me up some of his eggs and ham. He knew the best egg cookin' way. Momma2 was partial to boilin' eggs and eatin' 'em cold, so Zeke's hot cooked eggs was somethin' I was waitin' to get. I could've eaten a dozen of 'em. He always kept a ham in the smoker in the barn area, and he would just go out and cut off a slab to fry up with our eggs. He used the grease he saved in a coffee can to fry up his food. That bacon grease smell always made me think of Zeke.

I didn't knock when I got to his door. I just slipped in and said, "Zeke, could I eat breakfast with ya this mornin'?

He was sittin' in his chair with a tin cup of coffee in front of him. He didn't like me drinkin' it 'cuz he thought I was too little, but he knew I drank coffee with Momma2, so he asked me if'n he could fix me a little bit of brown brew? I said "yes" right away, feelin' like I had grown up in his eyes.

Zeke got a little fresh milk from Momma2 each day that he kept in a box packed with hay and cold water he drew up from his well. He had his own well outside his place that always had cold fresh water in it . He went over to the little box, pulled out the milk bottle, and poured my tin cup almost full of milk then added his brown brew on top. It looked like colored cream when he handed it to me, but I didn't fuss any about it 'cuz I knew his feeling about me and coffee. He gave me an old mason jar with sugar in it and a big table-spoon to dip in it. I took two heapin' spoons of sugar for my brown brew, mixed it up, and tasted it. I sipped on my drink and watched while Zeke got his old cast iron fryin' pan out of the oven of the cook stove and filled it with bacon grease.

My brown brew was more cold than hot on account of the cold milk, but it was right tasty. I watched as Zeke pulled some eggs out of another box he had tucked near the milk and watched him crack two eggs together and let them slide into the pan. He took two more eggs and did the same thing. He let the grease wrap around the whites of the eggs and make lace in the pan. They was fryin' while he went out and cut a couple pieces of ham and brought 'em in. He put the ham on our two plates then lifted the eggs hot and drippin' with grease out of the pan. My mouth was waterin' somethin' awful to get to tastin' 'em. He sat the plates down on the table then started to pray.

Momma2 wasn't the prayin' kind of woman, so we didn't hold to sayin' any kinda' prayer over our food, but when I went to Zeke's for breakfast, I had to bow my head and listen to him talk a bit 'fore I could put my fork in my food. Zeke's talkin' was always kinda sad soundin' like he was wishin' for somethin' he just couldn't have.

"I'm askin' you Lord to bless this food and make those'n of us that be eatin' it use it for good. Have mercy on us, Lord. We be tryin' our best to please ya. Amen."

I looked up at Zeke after he had his talk with his Lord then when I saw him lift his fork from his plate, as fast as I could, I did the same. He had a loaf of Momma2's bread on his table. He tore a hunk of it off for me to smear around my yolk. It was a fine breakfast, and I was thinkin' he musta been a fine husband to Belva to cook like he did.

Sometimes we talked, and sometimes we just ate. Today I wanted to talk, so I asked him how the orchard work was comin'.

"Well, Tilly Girl, I reckon we's gonna have us a mighty fine crop a apples if'n the weather holds out, and we keep up with our business. We's got us lots of baby apples poppin' out on them trees."

Zeke took his ol' red hanky and wiped his mouth. Seemed like everythin' needin' wipin' on him got taken care of with that ol' red piece of cloth. He stuck it back in his overalls then said, "Miss Kate be's the best help Miss Lila ever hired for ol' Zeke. She's be one hard workin' woman. How's her sister doin' with Miss Junie Bird?"

"Zeke, even though that Miss Essie Lou don't talk none, seems like she understands Junie Bird real good. They quilt like they's no tomarra. The box of ol' rags Momma2's been savin' is almost empty. She's gonna have to find some more to keep 'em goin'. Miss Essie done pukin'," I added, like he already knew. "So she's been helpin' Momma2 with the bread makin' and cookin' and cleanin'. Momma2 is plumb over the moon with all the help she been gettin' from her."

Zeke had a puzzled look on his face when he put down his fork. "Why's Miss Essie been pukin', Tilly Girl?"

"Well, I don't rightly know, only she was pukin' ever' day for a long time. I thought she'd puke up her guts, she puked so much. No sense in it, but she's done with that. Momma2 says she don't need Doc Gibbs."

Zeke got up from the table and brought his plate to the metal pan he had on a board by the stove. He came over and rubbed on my head. "Well there, Tilly Girl, life gets ta be hard on some people. Sure don't wish no bad on that pretty little girl."

"No bad will be comin' to her, Zeke, she's doin' good now." I picked up my plate and brought it over to the wash pan. Zeke used that pan for washin' his face and washin' his dishes. Now it was the dishes turn to get washed.

I went over to the cook stove and took the pot he kept on it to heat water. "Zeke, if you put a little of that hot water in the pan, I'll go pump some cold, then I'll wash your dishes."

Zeke put his hand on my shoulder. "Tilly Girl, go off now. Ol' Zeke'll get the washin' done in good time. I'm not in a hurry with em' today."

I put my arms around Zeke where I could reach and told him thank you for my breakfast then ran as fast as I could out the door. I decided, since I was at the barn, I'd explore the places I wanted to see while I was here.

The barn had window openings to let air get in, and when the light came through those window holes, you could see the dust sprinkle in the air like magic jewels. I loved to run through that shiny light and play like I was catching diamonds. I twirled and turned and giggled while I swept them dust pieces in my hands and let 'em go. I did that for quite a spell 'fore my legs got tired of runnin' in circles.

I walked over to the apple crates that was stacked high against the wall and counted 'em. I was good with my numbers. The crates was stacked higher than I could reach, but I counted as many as I could see with just my eyes. There was forty-two.

At the end of September, they'd all be full of apples. Momma2 would have someone from town come out with a big ol' truck and take 'em to the railroad station for the train to carry 'em off to sell. We'd use the money Momma2 got from the apples to make it to the next year. I was glad to hear Zeke say we was gonna have a good crop a apples.

The hay we bought for Ol' Bossy was stored in the barn, too. It was stacked in a big pile where mice liked to live and have their babies. I'd been lucky and found a nest of the little things a couple of times, so I knelt down on the floor near the hay and searched through some of it to see if I could find a nest again. I wasn't lucky today. While I was stirrin' 'round in the hay, a smell caught my nose that made me put my arm to my face. It was worse than the slop bucket smell. I knew a stink like that meant somethin' was rotten. Zeke would want to know what it was to get it out of the barn.

I stood up from the hay and started followin' the smell. I was walkin' round the corner of the stall that holds all the tools Zeke and Kate use off and on when my nose found the smell, and my eyes stared at what my nose had found.

I saw a little baby coon wrapped up by its neck hangin' on one of the tool hooks. Looked to me like it had been dead a good time 'cuz it's hair was all hard looking and it's little eyes was dried up and ate by ants or somethin'. It was real scary lookin', and I felt my stomach get that feelin' in it like it was gonna make me lose my breakfast. I tried to hold it in and ran to Zeke.

"Zeke, Zeke, come quick! There's a dead coon in the tool bin. It's rottin' somethin' awful and stinks to high heaven. Looks like it been hung up to kill!"

When I ran in on him, Zeke was standing by the wash-basin cleanin' our dishes. He put down the rag he had in his hand and reached for a flour sack towel Momma2 had had Junie Bird sew him to wipe his hands. He looked over to me with a frown on his face, and without saying a word, put the towel down. "Show me what cha talkin' 'bout chil."

I started to run, then I slowed down to keep in step with Zeke. We walked slowly to the tool bin, and when I showed him the dead coon, he put his hands to his mouth and covered it like it wasn't only the stink that was botherin' him but somethin' else. He walked over to the coon and untied his little neck. He carried it real careful like to the side of the barn and laid it down. Then, without sayin' any words to me, he went back to the tool room and brought out a shovel. He dug a little hole and laid the little coon in there like it was a human baby. He bent over it and covered it up real gentle like. Then he bent down on his one knee and said,"I's sorry fer ya' little coon—nothin' 'serves ta be hurt like you was hurt. You go on up to the Lord, now."

When he stood up, he took the shovel back to the tool bin. I followed him. His steps seemed heavier than when we was walkin' to the stinkin' smell. "Zeke, what you mean the coon was hurt? Who hurt him?"

Zeke took my hand in his big brown hand, and we walked for a few steps 'fore he said anything. "Tilly Girl, Zeke ain't sure who hurt that baby coon, but he sure didn't wrap that wire round his neck by hisself. Seems like we gotta be lookin' out for who done it. I 'preciate you showin' it ta me. That was right smart."

I didn't feel right smart—I felt right confused. How's come a baby coon was hangin' itself, or someone else was hangin' it? Didn't make a story to understand to me.

"You gonna tell Momma2 'bout that baby coon, Zeke? If'n you want I could tell her."

"Tilly Girl, you let ol' Zeke talk to Miss Lila 'bout that baby coon. Don't you be thinkin' bout it none."

I walked all the way to Zeke's place with him where he let my hand go with a pat to the top of it. You's go run and play, Tilly Girl, I's got's ta finish up them dishes we got messed up this mornin'"

I knew Zeke was tryin' to get me to stop thinkin' bout that little baby coon, hangin from a wire all rotten and ate up, but it was in my head, and it was gonna be there for a long time ta come.

Chapter 10

I could smell the chicken cookin' even 'fore I opened my eyes. The smell hung in the air around my bed like it was ready to drop a piece a chicken right in my mouth. I could hardly wait to get out a bed and get ready for the day.

It was July 4, and we was goin' ta town on a Friday. That made the day special even if'n it wasn't America's birthday. That's what Momma2 calls it. "Tilly, July 4, is America's birthday. We don't do no work on that day. We are all gonna celebrate."

Momma2 started in gettin' ready for this celebration most of the week. She made bread on Tuesday, leavin' a whole bunch of the dough out to fry up for sugar bread. She didn't make that very often and, when she did, you knew it was for somethin' special. She'd take a ball of dough and stretch it out like it was a piece of rubber, then drop it in lard and let it bubble up and fry away. She'd pull it out of the fat and drain it on old newspaper, then Momma2 would dip it in sugar to coat it good and sweet. It was made for eatin'.

Momma2 also made green bean salad with bacon and onions, and potato salad with radishes, spring green onions Essie Lou had pulled from the garden, and boiled eggs from our hens. Momma2's potato salad was so good it was the thing I wanted more than any of the other food. She only made it twice a year, once on my birthday 'cuz I always asked for it special and on July 4. I guess it was a good birthday food for sure.

This year Essie Lou asked Momma2 if'n she could make the pie for the picnic and, to my surprise, Momma2 said "yes." When I say Essie Lou asked Momma2, I don't mean like me askin' for somethin'. Essie Lou couldn't talk, so makin' Momma2 understand she wanted to make a pie wasn't the easiest thing I ever saw someone do, but when she pulled a pie pan from the shelf and pointed at it then pointed to herself, I guess Momma2 could figure it out 'cuz she nodded "yes," makin' Essie Lou reach out and hug Momma2. Momma2 wasn't too keen on the huggin' part, but she stood there real still like and let Essie Lou squeeze her' til she was done.

I wasn't too sure 'bout Essie Lou being the one to make an apple pie for our picnic. Essie Lou seemed kinda young to be makin' a pie all by herself without Momma2 doing some of it, but Momma2 didn't pay her no mind and just let her go at it like she knew what she was doin'. But I watched her real close.

Essie Lou went down to the cellar, all by herself, to get the apples from the dark place where the spiders might be. I was glad I didn't have to do that part. She picked out some green ones and some red ones, then she washed up the apples and laid 'em out in the kitchen ta dry. When the apples was good and dry, she went about makin' the piecrust. She seemed ta know what she was doing with that part. She cut lard into the flour and added salt and a little bit of sugar. To make sure the water was real cold and clear, she let the water run from the pump before she put it in the flour. She hummed a little while she was doing that. I didn't know how her mouth could hum when her words couldn't talk, but I figured her throat worked better than her tongue.

Essie Lou's hum wasn't like Junie Bird's. Junie Bird hummed like her mind was a motor. Essie Lou's hum made a sound like music—it was soft and beautiful. While I watched her in the kitchen cookin' and hummin' away while Momma2 was busy doing some of the gardenin', I thought Essie Lou shouldn't have had a bad accident 'cuz she was too pretty and nice to be hurt in any way. But I knew she had been 'cuz she still didn't talk any.

Momma2's kitchen was full of all the stuff ya needed ta cook. Essie Lou found the place to roll the crust and cut and slice the apples. She cut so many apples I thought they was gonna topple over in the pan, but they didn't.

When the pie was covered with the top piece of crust, Essie Lou wiggled her finger for me to come over. I crept over real soft like'cuz I weren't sure what she was needin'. When I got to the butcher block where she was fixin' on the crusts, she pointed at strips of dough she had cut. She looked at me with her big brown eyes, then she smiled and winked. That means she closed one of her eyes like it was talkin' to me in a teasin' kinda way. She held up one of her fingers like a signal to watch her. She took the strip of dough and twirled it around her finger like it was a string, then she laid that strip of dough 'round the edge of the pie like a lace collar. She took another strip and did the same thing 'til the edge of the pie was covered. Then Essie Lou did the silliest thing. She leaned over to skinny down her eyes to mine. She was actin' like there was a big secret comin' out of her which I knew she couldn't say. She took a tiny piece of dough and believe it or not, she made a flower out of it. It looked like an apple tree flower. It was the darndest thing. She put a little bit of water on the bottom of it, then she put it on top of the pie. She cut little holes for the air to breathe out like they was leaves comin' out of the flower, then washed it all over with egg wash, and put it in the oven. She patted my shoulder when she was finished to let me know she was done with me watchin' her. But I wasn't finished. She made me wonder even more 'bout her.

Essie Lou had no words, but she seemed to let ya know what she needed and how she needed it. And she didn't need much. She mostly just quilted and played with Junie Bird and helped Momma2 in the house and the garden. Ever' night, Essie Lou could hardly wait for Kate to get home from the orchard. I knew that 'cuz she started watchin' the door ta see if Kate was comin' through it when it was almost quittin' time for the orchard work. I could see her happy when she saw Kate come through the door. They was the best sisters ever.

The Putter twins coulda learned a thing or two from them 'cuz they mostly fought with one another. Zeke was always havin' to make 'em knock it off. Just the other day, I heard Ronnie poundin' on Remy in-between the trees. I don't know what was the reason, but when I saw Zeke comin' down the row, I knew they was gonna have ta stop their nonsense. Zeke didn't take no nonsense!

Two Saturdays ago, when we all went ta town to get supplies, Essie Lou bought material from Mr. Tribble. She picked out some red and some blue material. Each one of 'em had some design on it that made it look real pretty. She got some white lace and some thread, and Kate gave her money from her earnin's in the orchard to pay for 'em. I could see how happy that material made Essie Lou. She spent the next two weeks fussin' with it. She cut out newspaper pieces to fit up Junie Bird's shape then used an old shirt of mine to cut another. I don't know how she got Momma2's and Kate's, but when she was finished, she had each of us a new 4th of July wearin' outfit. Momma2 and Kate each had a shirt, and Junie Bird and Essie Lou each had a dress with a twirling skirt and cutout sleeves. Junie Bird's was fitted to her body like a glove. It made her look like a schoolgirl. Essie Lou's dress was loose fittin', but she could still twirl around with the air makin' the skirt on the dress whip around in a circle like a tent. Hers was blue and matched Kate's shirt and Junie Bird's was red and matched Momma2's shirt. Mine was red and blue and was the first dress I ever owned. The top of it was red with blue sleeve straps and the skirt was blue with red trim on the edge. When I put it on, I could whirl around and make a full circle with my skirt. It felt like I was one of them Malcolm girls all fancied up. Essie Lou even made me a bow to go in my hair with white lace all around it, but the bow didn't stay put, so it ended up in Junie Bird's braids.

Momma2 use to say, "Tilly, quiet waters run deep', meanin', I 's'pect, that you can't hear what's under ever'thing. That was true 'bout Essie Lou. You sure 'nough couldn't hear her talkin', but her heart worked out loud. Ever'body loved the new clothes. Junie Bird was twirlin' 'round like a doll all up in her happy place. I have ta say I was up there, too.

Momma2 was right pleased. She took Essie Lou's hand and held it real tight when Essie Lou gave us all our new 4th of July fittin's. "Essie Lou, it was right nice of you to make all these clothes for us. We're right thankful. And Kate," Momma2 turned to Kate when she added her name, "it was right nice of you to spend your workin' money on material for these new things. It's real nice havin' you two girls here with us."

I could see Momma2's eyes get wet, but she didn't let any of her tears fall from her eyes. But, Kate and Essie Lou wasn't so good at that. They both had streams of water roll down their faces when Momma2 talked so nice about 'em.

With our new clothes, Momma2's good cookin', and Essie Lou's best apple pie, we was fixin' ta have the best 4th of July picnic in Benton County. It was gonna be a remember forever day.

Momma2 wrapped all the cold stuff in hay and newspaper to keep it cold and she made a big glass jar of sweet tea. Then she put plates, glasses, and silverware together and packed up all the picnic stuff in a big wood box. On top of the box, she put a blanket that we was all gonna sit on when we wanted ta eat.

Zeke came up ta the house, on account of he was gonna load the 'ol truck for us. That's when Kate came out and asked Momma2 if'n we could drive her fancy red car ta town for the parade and picnic. Momma2 looked over to Kate like she was crazy.

"Now, Kate, why in Heaven's name would we do that? That car could barely hold all of us, let alone the box of picnic food. The truck will be just fine for today." She didn't let Kate talk any more about it. She just yelled over to Zeke to get the ol' truck loaded up for us. Zeke lifted the picnic box in the back. I was standin' by the ol' truck in my new twirlin' dress ready to hop in.

Zeke never went ta town for celebrations 'cuz that's when darkies ended up in trouble with white men that would get ta drinkin' too much, then get ta thinkin' they was the boss over ever' darkie that was around. Zeke didn't want none of that trouble business, so he stayed home and had some time ta himself. 'Sides that, Siloam Springs was a sundown town, like the rest a Arkansas. It didn't cotton ta any darkies pokin' 'round town after the sun went down, and we was gonna be gone way past sundown. Zeke would be in real trouble then.

"Fore we got in the truck to start our day, Essie Lou brought out a package for Zeke all wrapped up in newspaper with a pretty piece of lace tied on it for ribbon. She handed it to him with her eyes lookin' at him and her mouth not sayin' a word.

"Well, what's ya gots here, Miss Essie Lou?" Zeke took the package and held it for a minute. Kate answered for her.

"Zeke, Essie Lou made you something. We hope you like it. We appreciate how good you've been to me." I liked listenin' ta Kate talk in her Yankee voice. It sounded real strong and important.

Zeke smiled real big at Kate, then looked really shy like over to Essie Lou. "Now yous don't need ta be thankin' Zeke for being good. Goods how we's all s'posed ta be, ain't we?"

Zeke asked that question and then bowed his head and pulled the lace ribbon off the newspaper. As he unfolded the paper, six new hankies fell out of the package. One new hanky for ever' day of the week. They was red and blue, just like our new clothes.

Zeke's eyes couldn't hold the water from 'em. He took the hankies in his hands and put 'em up to his head like they was gonna be wipin' 'way his sweat. "These gonna make ol' Zeke look right smart out on his tractor workin' 'way Dixie land. Yous makin' ol' Zeke real happy with these new handkers. I's be thankin' y'all."

All three of 'em was kinda shy actin' after that. Zeke folded up his new handkerchiefs and put the newspaper and lace in his pocket. I was pretty sure he wasn't gonna be puttin' that paper in the cook stove to burn. I was bettin' he'd have it on his table for rememberin'.

Junie Bird, Kate, and me piled in the back of the truck with the box of picnic food, and Essie Lou and Momma2 piled into the front of the ol' truck. Momma2 drove, and the three of us watched as the road flew past us on the way to Siloam Springs.

When we entered the town, I could feel the excitement in the air. As we drove past the city limit sign, there was a banner across the road with "July 4, Independence Day" printed on it. There were red, white, and blue flags flying off each side of it, and all down the streets they had American flags stuck in flag poles making us remember we was celebratin' America's birthday. The town park was loaded with people, and the gazebo on the town green was all decorated with red, white, and blue streamers. The mayor was plannin' on makin' a speech 'round noon in that gazebo 'cuz he did that ever' year.

The carnival came ta town durin' the 4th of July time, and it was already set up near the park. I could see the Ferris wheel from the back of the truck, and I was anxious ta ride it. Usually, I had ta ride it with Junie Bird and listen ta her scream all the way up and all the way down. I was hopin' today ta get Momma2 to ride the Ferris wheel with me and let Junie Bird ride with Essie Lou.

We parked the ol' truck by the park and let the box of food stay in the truck. We all got out and started our walk over to the Main Street.

Siloam Springs had a Main Street with all its important buildin's on it. The street was wide, and the dirt on it was packed down hard from the cars goin' over it ever' day. Mr. Tribble's General Store was at the far end of the street where the parade was gonna be startin'. We headed that way.

Siloam Springs had a parade on the 4th of July' ever year and ever' year since I can remember, Junie Bird and me waved our little American flags with all 48 stars on it. Momma2 got these little flags at Mr. Tribble's when I was a baby, and she drug 'em out ever' year for us ta wave at the parade. All five of us took a place on the sidewalk in front of Mr. Tribble's store waitin' for the parade ta start down the road.

When I looked 'round at the people standin' waitin', I felt proud of my new dress and the way we all looked, so bright in our red, white, and blue birthday clothes. I saw the Malcolm girls standing near the bank with their momma and daddy, but they didn't see us. They was dressed in lacy white dresses with red and blue bows in their hair. They was sure 'nough in their fancy dressin' again. They musta had more clothes than a general store to have so many dresses ta chose from.

I heard the band and turned ta look at it start its marchin' down the street. The American flag was flying right in front of the whole mess of marchin' band. The soldiers that was carryin' the flag looked old and worn out, but they carried that flag like they was still full of muscle and guts. I knew I was suppose to put my hand over my heart when the flag marched by 'cuz Momma2 made me do it each year. She didn't make Junie Bird do it, though, 'cuz that's not somethin' Junie Bird wouldn't a got the hang of.

There was four soldiers marchin' across the front of the band with the flag, and then there was a baton twirler behind 'em spinnin' a baton and throwin' it high in the air and catchin' it. She spun around and let that baton hang in the air, then, when it came down, she was right there ready ta catch it and throw it up again. She made it look easy, but I knew it wasn't 'cuz I'd tried to throw a stick and catch it. It wasn't easy to know where it was gonna land when I tossed it up in the air, and I didn't even get it as high as that girl tossin' her baton. She was a marvel.

I could hear Junie Bird hummin' in her happy place and sayin', "Looky, Momma, looky!" She was pointin' at the girl and the band and sayin' " Looky, looky!" She said it ever' two minutes like we wasn't all lookin' just like she was. Essie Lou and Kate was lookin', too, and I could see smiles on their faces like they was likin' all they could see. They looked right nice standin' there watchin' the parade.

Kate's black hair was 'specially wavy, and her face looked like the sun had kissed it. She didn't put on any lipstick, but her lips was as red as cherries. Essie Lou was getting' fatter; it made her look even prettier than she did when she first got ta our place. Her cheeks was all filled out, and it made her eyes look like they fit her face. Both sisters was pretty—they was just different pretty.

Momma2 looked like she was havin' the time of her life. She was clappin' to the band music and singin' the songs she knew when they played them. Essie Lou had Junie Bird's hand and was not lettin' her go. Momma2 saw Essie Lou watchin' over Junie Bird, and smiled at Essie Lou with a big wide grin she didn't normally give anyone.

The Confederate flag came marchin' by, next with a group of eight men in ol' raggedy uniforms from the Civil War. I saw Kate and Essie Lou look at Momma2, but Momma2 just stared straight ahead then lowered her eyes when the group marched past. Some of the people watchin' the parade woo-hooed like them soldiers were their favorite part of the parade. When the soldiers passed us, Momma2 turned to Kate and Essie Lou, "The South is stubborn about the war. They had a hard time losin', and some people don't like to let go. You're Yankees, so you can't know how they feel, but some of these people still hold on to old beliefs. I wish they didn't."

I wasn't sure how come Momma2 took to preachin', but Kate and Essie Lou both listened, and then Kate took Essie Lou's hand. Essie Lou looked like she was gonna cry which made Momma2 take charge of what was happenin'. "Hey there now, this is America's birthday. The finest day of the summer. Let's finish watchin' the parade, then let's go grab us somethin' ta eat."

The parade wasn't that much longer. A few boys in scout uniforms and a couple of cars with pretty girls sittin' in 'em drove by, then a small group of soldiers marched past with a coffin draped with an American flag for us to remember the ones who fought so's we could be free. That's what Momma2 told me anyway, 'cuz last year I asked her who died, and she said, "Tilly, lots of folks died so's you and I could stand here and do what we want. You never forget that girl, you hear me?" I didn't forget it, and we all put our heads down when it went by real quiet like with our hands over our hearts.

When the parade had passed, the crowd of people started headin' for the park. We followed the crowd, makin' our way to the ol' truck. Kate and Momma2 pulled out the picnic box and brought it over to a place by the gazebo.

That gazebo had been built even 'fore Grandpa Poe was born. It's where the mayor was gonna stand when he talked to the town at noon. We got us a good listenin' place to sit. Essie Lou helped Kate and Momma2 spread out the blanket and put out the food. I could hardly wait to get to eat. I was 'specially anxious to get into that potato salad and chicken. Momma2 had left some of the food for Zeke, and I knew he'd be eatin' it at his table in his house or he might be eatin' it under a tree, makin' himself his own picnic.

I was sorry Zeke couldn't be here with us. I knew it had to do with them Confederate soldiers who marched by in the parade, and it wasn't makin' me like 'em for keepin' Zeke out of town on America's birthday.

Junie Bird couldn't sit still and was up runnin' around the park playin' with the air. Nobody paid her much mind on account a most people knew she was not right in the head. Some people pointed at her and some of 'em laughed, but I was learnin' my lesson to not be a low person and pay 'em no mind, too. That part wasn't easy.

I watched Essie Lou follow Junie Bird with her eyes and, when Junie Bird went too far away, Essie Lou got up and walked over to her, took her hand, and brought her back. Junie Bird followed Essie Lou like a baby calf followed ol' Bossy. When they got to the blanket, Essie Lou showed Junie Bird how to sit down and she did. Momma2 filled Junie Bird's plate with food. We was all kinda surprised when she started eatin' like a regular person. We lay on the blanket and watched people walk by. Kate told stories about the 4th of July in the North. It didn't sound much different than here 'cept they didn't have no Confederate marchers. We listened to people talkin' on their blankets in the park, while we ate the food Momma2 had packed for us. We saved the Essie Lou pie for later 'cuz our stomachs was full and we wanted to taste it all by itself.

The mayor got up at noon to talk in the gazebo. He looked real important standin' in the middle of that place with all its decorations hangin' 'round it like a birthday cake.

Ever'body in the park stopped talkin' and listened to him talk 'bout all the good things happenin' in Siloam Springs, 'specially some chicken man name a Simmon, who came to bring work for the people. Ever'body clapped for that. Then Mary Beth Hanson came up to stand by the mayor to sing *America* and *The National Anthem* and we all joined in. That is ever'body 'cept Essie Lou and Junie Bird. Junie Bird just wandered with her eyes in her never-never place, and Essie Lou stood with her hands folded listenin' to the music with her hand near Kate's. I saw Kate take Essie Lou's hand once and pet it really soft like. Essie Lou just smiled at the hand Kate was touchin'.

Kate, Junie Bird, and me played in the water runnin' down the park, danglin' our feet in and lettin' the water rush over our toes. The sides of the creek had been rocked up to make sure it was closed in and not leakin' on the park grass. It looked real pretty that way. It had a couple of bridges goin' over it in different places, and I run across 'em back 'n forth squealin' like I was bein' chased, but I wasn't. It was a hot afternoon, and my new dress was lettin' the air get underneath me and cool me down. Made me wonder why I never thought to wear a dress 'fore today. But I never had one before.

Momma2 sat on the blanket watchin' us. I saw her lift her glass of sweet tea up in the air and look at the glass for a while, 'fore she took it to her lips. I was wonderin' what was in the glass, her starin' at it like that. Maybe Momma2 didn't have lots of time to just look at a glass and, when she did have the time, she drank up on it.

People played and talked in the park, and I saw some of the people begin to head off ta the carnival. The carnival wasn't a far walk from the park, so we all took hands and headed there. Junie Bird was fightin' to go ahead of us 'cuz she wasn't wantin' ta wait to do the rides she remembered. Momma2 held her back.

There was plenty of people runnin' 'round the carnival booths, playin' the games, hittin' bottles over, spinnin' wheels, and tryin' to bang a hammer down to ring a bell. Ever'body was hopin' ta win some kinda prize.

Kate took to the game playin' like she was some kinda famous thrower. The first time I watched her throw the bags into the bottles, I thought the man behind the counter was gonna faint from surprise. Kate was knockin' them bottles down like they was matchsticks by the woodstove. She got ta pick a prize, but first, she looked at Essie Lou who turned ta look at Junie Bird who was jumpin' up with her hands by her cheeks. Kate turned to Junie Bird. "What would you like Junie Bird? How about that furry bear?"

The man behind the counter reached up to pick out a bear to hand to Junie Bird and when he handed it ta her, Junie Bird turned ta Momma2 wonderin' what she was s'pose ta do. Momma2 looked at her. "Go ahead Junie Bird. You can take it. Miss Kate won it for you."

I saw Momma2 turn and nod her head ta Kate like it was a thank you. Junie Bird reached for the bear and hugged it and squealed with a high joy that made people turn and look at her. I swear she was always doin' somethin' people thought needed lookin'.

Kate won another furry bear for me, then she started to do it again, but the counter man gave her a sour face and told her to give somebody else a chance ta win. I could tell he wasn't invitin' Kate back ta play.

We went ta other games ta play where Kate tried to help me win with my throwin,' but I didn't have the arm I needed to hit my mark. Kate won somethin' for Momma2, then, at the end of the night 'fore we all went ta the Ferris wheel, she won a big bunny for Essie Lou. I was thinkin' I wanted the bunny 'stead of the furry bear I got, but I didn't say nothin' 'bout it.

When we got ta the Ferris wheel, Momma2 said she'd hold all the prizes while we rode up in the wheel. That done messed up my plan ta ride with Momma2 instead of ol' Junie Bird. I was figurin' I was gonna be goin' up with her again, just like always, but when we got ta the front of the line, Kate reached over ta me. "How 'bout you and me go up and we let Essie Lou and Junie Bird ride together." I could hardly believe her words. This would be my first ride on the Ferris wheel with someone other than Junie Bird. I let Junie Bird and Essie Lou go first, and then me and Kate jumped on the next seat.

The Ferris wheel was painted with bright colors that showed off all its seats and the bars that held it together. When ya got up close ta it, you could see the paint chipped away in places, but that didn't bother me none 'cuz I was gonna get ta go up without Junie Bird sittin' beside me, feelin' like I had to watch her like a hawk bird.

When Kate and I climbed in and the kid workin' the wheel pushed down our bar, Kate looked down at me and said, "To the top of the world we go, Miss Tilly."

As the wheel started up, I looked at Junie Bird and Essie Lou in front of us and thought this would be the first time Junie Bird got ta ride with someone else, too. Essie Lou was for sure her good friend and Junie Bird didn't even know it.

The wheel creaked up and the chair swung in the air makin' me feel a tight scare in my stomach. I was wonderin' if'n Kate had those goosey feelin's, too, but when we got to the top of the wheel and was lookin' down on the whole town of Siloam Springs and seein' all the lights the night had to give us, I saw Kate take her hands off the bar and put her hands in the air, freein' herself from the only thing that held us in. That made my stomach feel like it was gonna lose the chicken and potato salad for sure. Kate was braver than anyone I knew to do that. As the wheel dropped from the sky, she let out a yell that echoed into the night. I grabbed the bar with both of my hands, afraid to let go, but my mouth let go of all scare I had been feelin'. We was both screamin' out ta the night in a way that let the night know we was both there. And it weren't the Junie Bird kinda screamin' we was doin' either—it was the kind that was full a fun! When we got to the bottom and started back to the top again, Kate looked over to me and gave me a squeeze with one of her free arms. I felt her warmth and knew what safe meant. Kate made me feel safe and I was bettin' she made her sister feel safe, too. Essie Lou was lucky.

We ended our ride, then Kate asked if we wanted some cotton candy. That was a question didn't need no answer. I ran toward the little booth that swirled with pink fluffy sugar makin' my mouth water to see it. We walked 'round with our candy as our mouths turned all pink and sticky. Momma2 just followed us, lettin' Kate lead us from one place to the next. It was gettin' dark when we finally finished playin' our last game. We walked back to the blanket to finish our picnic food and eat Essie Lou's apple pie while we waited for the fireworks ta start.

The pie was meltin' in my mouth. I told Essie Lou she sure did know how ta make a pie 'even if'n she wasn't as smart as Momma2 in the kitchen. Kate and Essie Lou both laughed at what I said, but Momma2 didn't look like what I said was so funny for 'em ta laugh at.

After we ate our dessert, we put all our food in the box and took it back ta the truck, then we got in the truck and watched the sky explode with the fireworks that looked like candles in the sky. It was America's birthday, and we was all celebratin' it. As the third firework went high in the air and broke out in sprays of colored lights, I saw the Putter twins walkin' 'round the park smokin' on some kinda paper and actin' like they was big and important men.

I saw Kate turn to watch 'em, too. I didn't know why her face turned dark, but I saw it and knew she wasn't fond a seein' 'em. They just wasn't the two people your eyes wanted ta fall on after you spent such a good day celebratin'.

I watched the back of Kate's head follow the twins 'til they was out in the night somewhere not in our eye view. She turned and saw me watchin' her. "Well, now Miss Tilly girl, that was a beautiful firework, wasn't it?"

I knew she wasn't watchin' a firework, and she knew I knew it, too, but I didn't say nothin' like that. I just nodded my head like we was lookin' and thinkin' about the same thing, and we was.

Chapter 11

The days following the 4th of July were hot and muggy. Momma2 kept sayin' the weather was weighin' her down. I didn't 'xactly know what that meant, but we was all sweatin' and wipin' water from our heads like we was just gettin' out of a bath. There didn't seem to be any relief from the heat. Arkansas heat was the kind that came on in the mornin' and set itself up for the whole day.

The orchard was hummin', just like Junie Bird, with a happy sound of all the work goin' on. Zeke had hired two more darkies, 'sides the Putter twins, to get the orchard work done. They was always trimmin' trees, diggin' the ditches to carry the water down the rows, and makin' sure all the weeds that wanted to choke out the trees was pulled out and burned in a pile. They was all sweatin' more'n any of us on account of 'em workin' in this damn blazin' heat.

Kate worked just like the men and wore herself out ever' day. When she came in at the end of the day, I could see she was wet from all her sweatin' while she was workin'. I guess the weather was weighin' her down, too.

One Sunday, after we ate our afternoon dinner, Kate asked Momma2 ifn' we could all go down to the creek to splash in the water to cool ourselves off. Momma2 said she thought that was a mighty fine idea, and she'd come down too. I was plumb surprised to hear that. Momma2 wasn't much on havin' fun.

Sager Creek was runnin' low in the heat of the summer, and there was plenty of places to rock up the water so we could play around in it. Kate, Momma2, and me found rocks to make a dam. We fixed it right tight to make the water hole up in it to make us a little swimmin' hole. Junie Bird and Essie Lou just sat on the bank of the creek and hung their feet in the water, lettin' the cold soak into 'em and cool 'em off.

When we got the hole rocked up and filled, Kate, Momma2, and me went right in and sat down. It was like a big old bathtub for all of us to sit in 'ceptin' we all had our underwear on. Momma2 and Kate both took off their shirts and pants when we got down to the creek. I let my eyes catch that sight a minute just ta make sure it was Momma2 I was seein' actin' like she was a youngun' . We laughed and hollered and splashed water and, 'fore we knew it, we was all soakin' wet from our head to our toes. I never heard Momma2 laugh so much, and she was splashin' water, just like me. I couldn't imagine Momma2 ever being a kid, but this time, in the swimmin' hole with her, gave me a picture of her I hadn't had before. She was right playful.

When I looked over at Junie Bird and Essie Lou, I could see Essie Lou smilin' a big pretty smile watchin' us play. She didn't seem to want to get herself in the water, but she sure seemed to like gettin' her feet cold. Junie Bird was lettin' her head bob up and down to the sound of her head hummin. She made her own music, I guess. Essie Lou never let Junie Bird out of her sight; that seemed to help Momma2 relax even more. I couldn't let myself think about the time when the orchard work was done and Kate and Essie Lou would have to move out of the slave house, take their fancy red car, and drive away. I was thinkin' they was becomin' family just like Zeke.

We spent a good chunk of the afternoon just playin' in the water. When we was tired of all that, Momma2 and Kate put their clothes back on, and we walked back up the trail to the slave house. At the slave house, Kate and Essie Lou waved their good byes and went inside.

The slave house had changed since they moved in. Essie Lou had sewn curtains for the windows. They was white with little flowers on 'em. They made the house look like the dwarf house in *Snow White*.

I s'pose Kate and Essie Lou musta worked around the house after work 'cuz there was flowers planted all 'round and they was bloomin'. There was also all sorts of fixin' goin' on. The tar patches had been changed to little wood patches and Essie Lou musta painted little decorations on 'em. They had found all kinda rocks 'round the place that they used to make a rock path right up to the porch steps and little round rock circles with wildflowers planted in them. I was thinkin' I could really play house in it now. They was real clean sisters, so the porch was swept off and the windows was sparklin'. You could see they was glad to have the slave house as their own home.

As we started down the path to our house with Junie Bird skippin' like she was little, Kate yelled out to us. "Momma2," she said, then caught herself coughing into her hand like she didn't really say that. "Miss Lila, excuse me, there's some rope and boards in the barn. If you don't mind, I could fix up a swing for Tilly in that big old tree. It looks like it needs a reason to hang on and a swing might be just the perfect fit for one of its limbs. Would you mind me doing that?"

I stopped and listened for Momma2's answer. I was hopin' it was gonna be a big fat "yes." I never had a swing, but I had seen 'em in the schoolyard and was thinkin' that was a fine idea for the Eve tree.

"Kate, if you can make that happen, I'm fine with it. I can imagine Tilly might like that. 'Course, you and Essie Lou might like it, too."

Momma2 waved good-bye and then prodded my shoulder to turn around and head for the house. I was so full of the afternoon fun and the thought of a swing of my very own, I started skippin', too. *"Won't wonders never cease"* is what popped into my head.

Ever' day, after that Sunday, I walked down to the slave house to see ifn' Kate had got the wood and rope up for a swing on the Eve tree, but I'm guessin' she was too damn busy 'cuz it didn't get up 'til the followin' Sunday. That day, she and Essie Lou come up to the house and told me it was ready for the first swingin', and I got to be the person to see ifn' it worked.

I walked in-between the two of 'em down to the Eve tree and there, hangin' like the best thing in the world, was a swing. I don't know how Kate got up to the high limb to tie the ropes, but I didn't care how 'cuz they was all tied up hangin' there with a board at the bottom ready for me to sit and swing.

Kate and Essie Lou watched while I climbed on, then Kate gave me a push into the air. I felt the wind rush by me on that hot day and tasted the breeze it made. It was even better than the Ferris wheel. Kate kept pushing me and told me to bend my legs back and forth, then I could keep goin' on my on. It took me a few tries, but pretty soon, I was makin' that swing go up in the sky like a bird flying through the air. It was the best feelin' in the world! As I swung through the air, I could see Kate and Essie Lou below me smiling big and wavin' at me like I was goin' somewhere. I didn't take my hands from the ropes 'cuz I wasn't too sure ifn' I'd fall out, so I just yelled "hello" to 'em from up in the air, so they could hear how much fun it was. I thought maybe I could spend my whole life swingin', but my legs got tired after a while, so I let the swing slowly stop and I got off.

When my feet hit the ground, they started walkin' straight to Kate. I couldn't even believe what I did when I did it, but sure enough, I hugged her around her middle and said, "Thank you, Kate. This is the best thing in the whole wide world!"

I felt her hand on my head and, when I looked up at her, I could see her smile and the wet eyes she was so good at showin' when she was too happy for words. She patted my head. "You're welcome, Tilly. That tree was begging for someone to love it, and now it's got a playmate. I'm sure it will have new life because of you."

I never saw the Eve tree like I saw it that day. It looked like a new friend to me—one that was strugglin' to stay alive, but now it had a brand new swing swingin' from its branch that made it look happy to me. Kate and Essie Lou returned to the slave house, and I stayed to swing on my swing. Soon, I heard Momma2 call me in for Sunday dinner, so I ran down to the slave house to tell Kate and Essie Lou. I knocked on their door and yelled, "It's Sunday dinner. Time ta eat." Then I ran like the wind back to the house. As I started to run past the Eve tree and the swing, I stopped. I looked up at that ol' tree and my swing hangin' from it. I put my arms in the air like I was huggin' both of 'em and I 'pect I was, I was that happy.

Ever' day I did my chores then ran over to play with my new friend, the old Eve tree and my swing. Junie Bird didn't have the brains to sit on the swing and not let go ifn' it was in the air, so Momma2 didn't let her get on it. I'm sure glad Junie Bird made me with brains. I wasn't wantin' to miss out on the fun.

On Friday afternoon, Essie Lou and Junie Bird brought out a blanket and put it under the Eve tree where they sewed on their quiiltin' pieces while I did my swingin' time. Momma2 was in the garden doin' some weedin'. I think I felt somethin' in the air before I saw the black cloud cover the sky, but when I heard Momma2 scream at us to get to the cellar, I knew we was in for a big storm.

Storms that made us go to the cellar didn't come very often. I was four the last time, and I didn't know they was spiders and crawly things down there then. Now, I knew them creepy crawly things was down there waitin' to get me and I didn't want to go. I saw Essie Lou pick up the blanket, take Junie Bird's hand, and start to run toward the cellar. She looked at me, but 'cuz her words didn't work, she waved her hand for me to come. I kept swingin' pretendin' not to see her. Her eyes was beggin' me to come while she was runnin' Junie Bird all the way.

When I saw Momma2, I knew I was gonna end up in the cellar with all of us crowded around waiting for the storm to pass. Zeke, Kate, the Putter twins, and the darkies would have to hide out in the orchard in the ditches. That's what the orchard workers did when they couldn't get to a cellar or basement. The ditches was good for keepin' 'em safe.

In March, a tornado had killed fifty people and injured over 300 more in some far off county in Arkansas, so Momma2 was probably thinkin' we was gonna be next ta die 'cuz, when I saw her comin' for me while I was still on the swing, I stopped swingin' and let myself drop ta the ground. She pulled me by the hand barely lettin' my feet touch the ground and jerked me down the stairs of the cellar.

When we was down there, I could hear Junie Bird hummin' her worried hum and I could tell Essie Lou was there, but I couldn't see neither one of 'em. We was just crowded in that cellar waitin' for somethin' to happen. After a while, my eyes got use ta the darkness, then I could make out the shapes of Junie Bird, Momma2, and Essie Lou.

Momma2 and Junie Bird was wrapped up together. I could see Momma2's hand pettin' on Junie Bird's head like she was tryin' ta calm her down. Pretty soon, Junie Bird stopped her hummin' and just let Momma2 hug onto her.

I thought I heard cryin', but I wasn't sure who was doin' it. I thought maybe it was Essie Lou. Her being a Yankee, she might not have storms like this, but I wasn't sure. I didn't want her scared, so I reached over to where I thought her hand was and took hold of it. She squeezed my hand lettin' me know she was there.

I kept myself worryin' over the crawly things that I knew was down there with us. I figured those damn ol' bugs could see us with their beadly little eyes that could see in the dark.

We sat there for a long time, longer than I could count the number, when I saw the cellar door open and heard Zeke. "Y'all come on up now—yous be safe. Just a big wind comin' through the heaven lookin' to land someplace else. We's all safe."

I could see Kate's face in the door beside Zeke, and Essie Lou saw her, too. I could see Essie Lou reaching up for Kate's hand and saw Kate grasp Essie Lou's hand and hold it up to her cheek. Essie Lou climbed the stairs, and when she was on the ground beside Kate, she reached for Kate and hugged her as tight as Momma2 was huggin' Junie Bird. Momma2 made Junie Bird feel safe and Kate made Essie Lou feel safe. Zeke and me, well, I guess we could just be safe by ourselves.

Momma2 looked over to Zeke. "How's the orchard? What's lost?" Momma2 had worry all over her face when she asked Zeke that question.

"Miss Lila, the Good Lord be lookin' afta yous, today. Ol' Poe be up there makin' sure yous OK. We don't lose nuthin' but a few lose sticks here and there. We's gets that all cleaned up fast as fast. Don't yous worry none, Miss Lila. Them Putter boys and them darkies ran off home. They's be back tamarrow when they's not so scared of their tails gettin' blowed off."

Zeke smiled at Momma2. She lowered her head, then looked back up. "Thank you, Zeke. I 'm glad ta hear that."

Momma2 looked over to Kate and Essie Lou. Essie Lou was still stuck in the crook of Kate's arm with tears runnin' down her cheeks. "Kate, take Essie Lou home. She's had quite a fright, and that isn't good for her, now. You let her rest tonight."

Seemed like Kate should a been the one ta rest since Essie Lou was in the cellar safe and sound, but Momma2 was worryin' over Essie Lou and was tellin' Kate to worry over her too.

"Yes, ma'am, Miss Lisa, I'll do that." Kate nodded at Momma2, then took Essie Lou's hand and they walked hand in hand on down to the slave house. It wasn't 'til they was out of sight I thought of my swing. I was bettin' that damn thing was stuck high in the Eve tree and we'd never get it down.

Chapter 12

I have no idea what woke me up, but I knew when I sat up in my bed and saw the lights on, it was somethin' pretty big to have a commotion goin' on in the middle of the night.

First thing I heard was cryin', and it weren't the kind of cryin' I ever heard before. It was the kind that sounded like some animal was trapped all up in a bad place and couldn't get out. I pushed the Junie Bird quilt off of me and jumped out of bed to yank open my door and see what was goin' on. Nothin' in the world could a made me 'pect to see what I saw next.

I was wipin' the sleepiness from my eyes when I saw Essie Lou holdin' on to Momma2, cryin' to beat the band. She looked like she was pullin' Momma2 down with her cryin'—pullin' on her to come with her. And she was talkin'. Not just cryin', but Essie Lou had words comin' out of her mouth and they wasn't Yankee words either. They was as southern as all a us. She was yellin' for Momma2 to come and help Kate. She was draggin' on her arm and pullin' her out the door.

Momma2 was in her nightgown and she didn't have no shoes on her feet. Essie Lou looked like she was worn out from what was goin' on with Kate. I heard Essie Lou sayin', "You's gotta save her fer me, Miss Lila. She's bad hurt!" I couldn't believe my ears was hearin' her talk like that, but they was hearin' 'xactly that. Momma2 didn't seem to think it was anything strange. She listened to her like she knew she had words to say.

Momma2 took Essie Lou's hand and grabbed a flashlight from the back porch so's she could see her way to the slave house. I don't think neither one of 'em noticed me followin' along like I was invited. Essie Lou was wailing the whole way, talkin' bout those boys maybe killed Kate. That's when my heart started racin' through my chest like it didn't want to stay there. I couldn't quite get the picture in my head about boys killing Kate. Which boys would they be and why would they be wantin' to hurt Kate? She was just about the nicest person I knew, next to Zeke and Momma2.

Momma2 tried to calm Essie Lou. "Don't you worry none, Essie Lou. We's gonna fix your sister just as soon as we get to her...don't be worryin' yourself or you're fixin' to make that baby you growin' get here 'fore it's suppose to.

I almost lost my footin' when I heard Momma2 talkin' about a baby growin' in Essie Lou. I seen her stomach gettin' big as a barrel, but I never figured there'd be a baby makin' it grow. She wasn't married to no man, and I knew enough about baby makin' to know you had to have a man around to make one. I couldn't figure out how that happened without me knowin'.

I heard Essie Lou answer Momma2 with a slow, low voice, "Miss Lila, Kate isn't my sister—she's my life and, if'n anything to happen to her, I don't want to live."

The dark of the night held all those words I just heard and put them in a place in me that made 'em a mystery. Kate hurt, baby growing in Essie Lou, Essie Lou talkin' like me, and then, they wasn't even sisters. I was followin' into a story I wanted to read.

I heard Kate groan as we got near to the slave house and, when Essie Lou heard her, she started runnin' to get to her. Momma2 followed and shined the light near where she heard Kate and Essie Lou. The light from the flashlight hit the Eve tree and the moss hanging off of it makin' all kind a shadows in the night. It looked beautiful standing there. It really was majestic and I knew right then why Momma2 couldn't chop it down. She loved that tree just like she had loved Grandpa Poe and Momma2 fought for ever'thing she loved.

As we came 'round the other side of the Eve tree, we saw Kate. Kate was tied to the Eve tree with ropes. Her body torn up like it had been raked over with a fork. Her black curls was matted to her head with blood that made it stick with its thickness. Her eyes were covered with the blood that had run from her head, and her nose looked like it was pushed to the side and not able to smell from the smashin'. I could see her lips was swollen so big she could barely make sounds come out of her mouth, and I could see the rest of her body was beaten up from somethin' I couldn't wrap my mind around.

Momma2 ran to Kate and she got right down ta business and started un-knottin' the ropes that was wound 'round Kate's body like she was a mummy. The knots must a been tied up pretty hard on account a it took Momma2 a extra long time to get 'em off of Kate. When she got the last knot undone, she yelled for Essie Lou to help her lower Kate to the ground. I could hear Essie Lou wailin' for Kate to be alright, but Kate was not able to say the words she wanted on account a her mouth was full of blood and her lips was too big to make the words.

As Momma2 and Essie Lou laid Kate down, I could see a handle of wood pokin' out a her bottom like it had been pushed inside her. I couldn't stop the tears from comin' out a my eyes. Miss Kate was hurt somethin' terrible and I could see why Essie Lou was thinkin' she was goin' ta die.

"Essie Lou," Momma2 said with a firm voice that wasn't a yell but sounded like she wanted Essie Lou to make sure she heard, "You listen to me and do as I say. You go get me some water and rags. You do that right now and don't be carrying on with your cryin'. Can't be cryin' when we gotta fix Miss Kate."

Momma2 had Kate on her lap and was cooin' to her like she was a little baby. "Don't you worry none, Kate, I gotcha, sweet girl. Nobody's gonna hurt ya now." Momma2 looked over to me. She spoke low and steady so as not to make me miss any of her words, "Tilly, take this flashlight and go get Zeke. Tell him to go to town and get Doc and do it right fast. Tell him to take you with him so's no one worries he's not doin' what I asked him to do. You run as fast as you can and get this done."

"Is Kate gonna be okay, Momma2?" I asked after she told me to go get Zeke. "Tilly, this is not the time for questions. It's the time for doin'. Now get to doin', and I mean now!"

I left Momma2 with Kate in her lap. I heard Essie Lou' s crying in the background as I headed up to the barn to get Zeke. I don't know if I ever been to the barn in the dark. It was right scary movin' through that ol' buildin' without the sunshine in it. As I run through the barn, my mind thought a that poor baby coon all tied up by its neck with its little baby eyes all bugged out and then I thought of Kate. I run faster and I yelled fer Zeke loud as my voice could let me.

"Zeke! It's Miss Kate! Somebody done hurt her real bad. She needs the doctor. We's gotta go get him right now!"

Zeke came out of his lean-to with his overalls on but no shirt. He didn't have no shoes on his feet neither. I told him again about Miss Kate. He didn't need nothing else said. We both ran to the truck and got in. He drove as fast as I ever rode in that ol' truck. Windows was down, and the wind felt like it was whippin' us as it came in. Zeke looked over to me, "Why's Miss Kate hurt, Tilly?"

I didn't know how to answer him 'cuz I really didn't know. "Don't know Zeke. She's got tied to the Eve tree with a broom stuck in her bottom. She's bleedin' all over herself, and Essie Lou is sayin' she might die." I began ta cry while I was sayin' all that cuz' I never saw anybody so bad hurt, and I was thinkin' she might die, too.

"Let that thinkin' go, Tilly Girl. We's gonna get doc ta fix her up good as new. Just be thinkin' that whilst we drive to get 'im." Zeke didn't know it, but I saw tears glisten in his eyes through the night sky. After I told him my story, he drove harder and faster.

Zeke had to pound on Doc Gibb's door for a good five minutes 'for the porch light came on and he opened the door. I was standin' by Zeke, just in case some Confederate wanted to tell him it was past sundown.

"Mr. Doc Gibbs," Zeke said with his head bowed down. "Miss Kate got hurt something terrible, and she's be needin' ya to look after her pretty fast. I's drive you there in the truck if'n you's want."

Doc Gibbs had been in Benton County since way 'fore I was born, even 'fore Junie Bird was born, so he knew not to be askin' questions if someone was hurt. If'n someone came ta get him in the middle of the night, then he knew somebody was hurt bad enough for him to get goin. He didn't change his clothes, just grabbed his doctor bag and climbed into the truck with me, sandwiched in the middle 'tween him and Zeke. As we started down the road, he started askin' questions.

Zeke couldn't answer none of his questions 'on account a he didn't see Miss Kate. I told him all I saw. He was quiet after that. When we got to our house, we all run to the slave house ta see what was goin' on there. I was scared I'd see Miss Kate dead to the world on the ground with Momma2 holdin' her. That ain't near what we seen.

Momma2 was still holdin' Kate, but she had a cool rag wipin' on her face and her lips. Kate was makin' sounds like Ol' Bossy moanin' when her baby calf was taken away. Essie Lou was kneelin' beside Kate wiping blood off her arms and neck. Doc Gibbs come up on 'em and let out a sound like wind through the trees, loud and long. It sounded like he emptied his lungs out a air.

"Let me see her, Miss Lila. Take care lettin' her head down."

Momma2 got up careful as a cat and lay Kate's head on the ground. Kate's eyes looked like they was scared of the world. Essie Lou wouldn't get up, so Doc Gibbs had to lift her with his arms to make her move away from Kate so's he could doctor on her.

Momma2 went over to Essie Lou and put her arms around her. It was then I noticed how big Essie Lou's belly was and for sure I knew she was growin' a baby inside. Essie Lou put her head on Momma2's shoulder, and I could see her body movin' up and down, keepin' with the cry that was comin' out of her. We was all cryin'—even Zeke.

Doc Gibbs took his neck tube to listen to Kate's heart. He listened real careful. We was all real quiet while he listened. When he was done listenin', he took real careful time feelin' all 'round over Kate. He felt her head and her neck then he looked real close to her nose. I could tell he didn't want ta touch it just yet 'cuz it didn't look like a nose, but a splash on her face. He checked inside her mouth and when he reached inside, Kate moaned a loud moan like she was being hurt again. That's when I thought about Essie Lou being hurt so bad she didn't talk. Now, Miss Kate wouldn't be talkin', and I could see why.

When Doc Gibbs got ta Kate's body, he felt ever' inch of it with careful touches. When he got ta the broomstick in her bottom, he looked over ta Zeke. "Zeke we gotta get this girl to Miss Lila's house, so I can fix her up. You think you can carry her?

I seen Zeke carry a ol' Bossy's calf like it was a little baby. He was strong and was full of muscles that worked hard. I knew he could carry Miss Kate and I knew he would do it real gentle.

Zeke nodded to Doc Gibbs, then he bent down beside Miss Kate. I seen the tears in Zeke's eyes fall on her as he put his arms under Kate and lifted her to his chest. The broom handle was stickin' out a her like a pole, but he lifted her so's it was hangin' down and not bein' in his liftin' way. As he pulled her to his chest, and I could see her head fall forward and rest on his overalls. There was nothin' stoppin' his cryin' then. His tears fell like the pump water out a his eyes. Zeke took little steps all the way to Momma2's house so as not to jiggle Kate none. Essie Lou, Momma2, and me was walking behind him and Doc Gibbs. When they got to the door, Momma2 said to put her down in her bedroom on her bed. Nobody even worried none about the quilt gettin' bloody.

When Zeke lay her down on the bed, the layin' down part musta hurt Miss Kate somethin' awful 'cuz she cried out, then Essie Lou started up again. She ran over to Kate and put her hand on her head. "Oh, Kate," she said so sad, I cried again hearin' her. "My darling, Kate. Please don't leave me."

Doc Gibbs took Essie Lou's hand and looked over to Momma2. I think it's best you take Miss Essie out of the room while I fix on Miss Kate. Best she not be here for all what's got to happen."

Momma2 looked over to me. "Tilly, you take Essie Lou to the kitchen and fix her a cup of hot cocoa. Don't come in this room 'til I come get ya. You hear me, girl? If'n Junie Bird gets up, you make her a cup of hot cocoa, too. She'll be fixin' to come in here if'n she knows I'm here, so don't be tellin' her nothin'. It's best that way."

Kate was too hurt for me to argue any, so I took Essie Lou's hand and told her to come with me. She pleaded to stay with Kate, but after some talkin, Momma2 convinced her to follow me and get a cup of cocoa.

When I got to the kitchen, I set the pan on the stove, took the milk jug out of the ice box and poured some in the pan. The stove wasn't as hot as it was in the mornin' when Momma2 got it goin' with new wood, but it was hot enough to get the milk warm. While it was gettin' warm, I pulled two cups out of the shelf under the sink and put spoons of cocoa and sugar in each of 'em. When the milk was good and warm, I used a ol' piece of rag to hold the handle, then I poured the milk in the cups and stirred it 'round to make sure it was gonna be good. I kinda felt like I was grown up makin' that hot cocoa all by myself. It was the first grown up thing Momma2 had asked me to do in the kitchen 'sides to do the chores I do.

I set the cups of cocoa on the table where Essie Lou was sittin'. She was still cryin', but her cryin' was soft soundin' now. I could see her face real clear now. She had a bruise that wrapped around her mouth and slipped into her blond hair. I hadn't noticed it 'fore now.

"Essie Lou, what happened to you and Miss Kate?" I asked it like I could find out the reason the sisters had been hurt. When she heard my question, she closed her eyes real tight like they was hurtin' and rocked her head back and forth tryin' ta get the reason out a her head. "Oh, Essie, I'm sorry ta ask ya that. Don't be answerin' or thinkin' on it. Just drink up your hot cocoa and let your baby know it's okay."

That's the first time I talked about her baby, but I was guessin', since Momma2 knew, she wouldn't mind me knowin'.

Essie Lou took her hot cocoa in her hands. Both of 'em. She held it still and looked over the cup to fix her eyes on me. "Tilly, I's so sorry you have ta witness such horrible things, young'un. This is more'un your eyes should see."

I thought on that for a minute 'cuz I was hopin' Miss Kate was gettin' fixed in the bedroom, then they'd be happy sisters again down at the slave house. "I'm okay, Miss Essie Lou, don't you worry none. I'm sure glad you be talkin' again. You ain't no Yankee though, like your sister. You's one of us people from the south. How's come your sister sounds like a damn Yankee?"

I didn't think about callin' Miss Kate a "damn Yankee," but it come out a my mouth 'for I knew it was comin'. Essie Lou looked at me for a long hard second. "Miss Kate's not my sister, Tilly. We come from different people. She comes from New York like she told y'all, and my people come from Kentucky. We met at work. We's just real close, like sisters."

That was good for me. I was wishin' I'd find a friend that would be close as a sister ta me, someday. I drank my hot cocoa so slow it was near cold when I finished it. I took my cup to the sink and washed it up so's Momma2 wouldn't have ta tell me what to do. I turned around when I heard Momma2 and Doc Gibbs come out of the room. Zeke must a stayed in the room with Kate.

"She can't be moved, Lila. Not for several weeks. She's gotta mend and that's gonna take some time. You think you can take on what she needs done to get better? It's not an easy job. I know the medicine I gave her will help some with the pain, but she's gonna be layin' in her own mess if'n you don't help her with her business. I suppose Essie Lou will help, too, but she can't be doin' any liftin this far along. You got your hands full with these two women at your house. You know that don't you, Lila? I'm gonna have to talk to the sheriff about all this business. Those boys are gonna have to be brought in for doin' this. No matter their reason. This here's a crime against a crime."

Momma2 was quiet as she listened to Doc Gibbs. When he was finished, she looked Doc Gibbs in the eye and said, "What you talkin' 'bout a crime against a crime?" She said loud and firm, holdin' onto the last word like it was fire on her tongue. "You talkin' like I think you talkin' Gibb? Those girls ain't causin' no crime—they just mindin' they own business, and that ain't no crime. You don't be tellin' the sheriff any tales now, you know what I'm sayin'? Cuz, if'n you fixin' on tellin' any tales on Miss Essie and Miss Kate, it be the last time I be askin' ya to my house. You hearin' me?"

Momma2 wasn't worryin' none that I was within hearin'. She just kept talkin'. "Gibb, you get those boys in jail and you throw away the key. There be something wrong with a person could do something like what they did. Don't be sayin' "it's a crime against a crime." Isn't but one crime and they's the ones that done it. We straight on that, now?"

Doc Gibbs took up his bag and looked up at Momma2. "We think different, Lila, but I'm a doctor and gotta live by my doctorin' promise. I'm fixin'

Miss Kate, and when the time comes, I'll deliver Miss Essie's baby. Don't have to like it. I'll just do it."

Momma2 put her arm around Essie Lou and pulled her close. "Too much hurt has been done 'cuz people think like you. You're a doctor, Gibb. You served in the war, and I know you seen stuff the rest of us never have ta see. I've known you a long time, and this is the first time I hear you talkin' like some of them crazy crackers down the road. I think more of you than them. Don't be makin' me think I'm wrong about who you are."

Momma2 stood with Essie Lou, then she looked over to me. "Tilly, we gonna be seein' the sun come up before we see the moon leave. I'm gonna be needin' you and Essie Lou to help me with Kate. We gotta get that girl better, so she can start workin' again."

Chapter 13

After Zeke drove Doc Gibbs home, he'd come back and stayed up all night by Kate's bedside. When the sun came up, he went to work in the orchard like he'd slept all night. Not one of us had slept and probably wouldn't until the night took on it's stars.

I'd been back and forth to Momma2's bedroom gettin' Kate's slop bucket emptied and bringin' cool water to her for sippin'. Her mouth was even more swoll up than last night, so I couldn't even tell where her normal mouth should have been. Doc Gibbs musta helped fix her nose last night while he was in the room with her 'cuz it had its shape back and there was cotton stuffed in it with little pieces of wood on each side and tape over the wood.

Kate looked like a monster from the Grimm's Fairy tale book I borrowed from the library. Her skin was black and blue and her eyes was closed shut 'cept for little slits to see a bit of light. Doc Gibbs had pushed pillows under her legs to lift her bottom in the air and Momma2 had put big ol' rags on her bottom like baby diapers to keep her from messin' herself. The pole stickin' out of her bottom was gone. I figured Zeke took it away someplace ta burn in the stick pile.

Essie Lou had stopped her cryin' and took to takin' care of Kate. She and Momma2 had worked back and forth to make sure Kate had water, cool rags on her head, and a clean diaper whenever she needed that.

I couldn't imagine Kate was likin' that diaper business 'cuz she couldn't be private 'bout anything goin' on with her, but she just laid there and let those two women do whatever they had to do. In the middle of the mornin', Essie Lou lay down on the bed next to Kate and fell asleep. Momma2 had told her to let that baby get some sleep, and that musta done it 'cuz she went out like a light bulb.

When Junie Bird woke up in the mornin', she was her ol' dumb self and didn't have no idea of the night's happenins.' She just went 'bout the mornin' like it was a regular ol' day, ate her breakfast then went over to her quiltin'. I don't even think she gave a thought to Essie Lou not bein' with her. She was like that. Didn't make yesterday any of today's business. She just lived whatever was happenin'.

Since Junie Bird couldn't see Kate and Essie Lou in Momma2's bedroom, she just didn't even think about 'em. I heard her hummin,' so I went and done my chores. When I came back in, Momma2 was in the kitchen gettin' her mornin' work done. She wiped her hands on the kitchen rag then looked over ta me. "Tilly, come in here and sit down."

Momma2 never told me to sit in the kitchen in the middle of the mornin' which made me tilt my head over like I didn't hear what she said right. "Come on, sit down here, Tilly, I gotta talk ta you 'bout some things."

I was wearin' the dress overalls Essie Lou had just made for me with the big pockets with colored material. I put my hands in those pockets, walked over to the table, and put myself on the bench I usually only sat on to eat my meals.

I could tell Momma2 was holdin' worry in her. Her hair was uncombed from last night, but she had put daytime clothes on and put her nightgown that held Kate's blood in the dirty basket. Her face had lines in it that pushed the worry up to her eyes. She put her elbows on the table and folded her hands like she was prayin', but I knew she wasn't the prayin' type. I sat there and waited for her to talk. She took a big breath of air and let it out 'fore she got goin'.

"Tilly, this isn't easy for me ta tell ya, but we may have some trouble comin' to us, and I need you ta know what's goin' on. Here it is, all laid out for ya.

Some of it's not goin' to be somethin' you'll understand, so if'n you've got questions whilst' I'm tellin' ya, I s'pect ya to ask me and I'll 'splain ta ya what I can."

I watched her run her hands through her hair and twist at a piece of it 'fore she started.

"Tilly, first off, those Putter twins was the ones hurt Essie Lou and Kate. They's got troubles for themselves and brought trouble to us. I didn't see it comin' the way it did, but when Zeke told me 'bout that dead baby coon, I shoulda known it was them and they was up to no good. They just got meaner by the year."

"Them boys musta been sneakin' 'round the slave house peekin' in on the girls. Maybe wantin' ta see how pretty they was at night. Now, this part's the part that's hard to tell on. " Tilly," Momma2 stopped and put her eyes right on mine. She wasn't starin' at me, but her eyes looked like they was drillin' into me deep inside and her voice had the low sound made me listen real good. "Kate and Essie Lou aren't sisters. They love each other like I loved your Grandpa Poe."

Momma2 stopped talkin' for a minute then turned to look over to the sink area where the window was. I was thinkin' on what she had said. "Momma2, you sayin' Kate and Essie Lou love each other like you loved Grandpa Poe? Is that truth you sayin' 'cuz, if'n it is, I don't know how that is. How can that be?"

I could tell this was a trouble answer for her 'cuz she tilted her head down, then looked back at me. "Tilly, when I met your Grandpa Poe, I had a feeling come over me that I can't explain. I knew he was gonna be in my life and sure enough he was. I loved him deep inside and I don't have words to tell you how that was. But it was. And, Tilly, I'm hopin' someday you'll meet someone just like your Grandpa Poe and love that person with that deep love. Kate and Essie Lou feel the same way 'bout each other. It's just love, plain and simple. The laws say they aren't suppose to love each other 'cuz they are both girls, but, Tilly, sometimes the law is not right.

"Once upon a time, Zeke and other darkies was bought and sold like ol' Bossy. Darkies didn't even have a say to where they went and how they was treated. Some of their children was sold away from 'em, and the law said it was alright."

Momma2's voice was gettin' quiet, but it held a hard edge. "That law was wrong, and the law telling Kate and Essie Lou that they can't love each other is wrong, too. And because of that law, we might be havin' some trouble at our house."

"Now I want you to remember something and remember it good, nothin's ever wrong with love, Tilly. Just 'cuz people say it's wrong don't make it wrong. Kate and Essie Lou never hurt nobody, but they been hurt plenty just 'cuz they love. I want ya to know that's the part that ain't right. Essie Lou got hurt in the last place they lived 'cuz some men at her work thought she should love them instead of Kate. That's why she's carryin' a baby. The poor girl didn't do a thing wrong, and they hurt her for lovin' Kate. Essie Lou and Kate come to Siloam Springs to get away from the hate and had to tell us they was sisters 'cuz they was afraid a what we might think."

The quiet in the air between us was broken by Junie Bird and her damn hummin'. I turned to look at her. She was just sittin' there with material in her lap, her sewin' needle goin' in and out with the sound of her hum. Seemed like she was kinda lucky not havin' to worry on some of the life stuff. I turned back ta look at Momma2 and saw tears shinin' in her eyes like they was ready ta fall down, but she held on ta 'em tight until they dried up.

Momma2's voice was shaky when she started in talkin'. "Tilly, not ever' body thinks like me. Doc Gibbs has been my friend for a long time. He done brought you into the world when Junie Bird's time come, and he come out to fix Kate. I owe him for the good he done for me and my family. But if'n Doc Gibbs brings Sheriff Joe inta our business, he and I might have to part our friendship and things might get ugly. I want ya ta know what's happenin' 'fore it might. You understandin' me?"

I was tryin' really hard ta understand, but they was too many new things to put in my mind for all the understandin' I needed, so I just nodded my head.

"Momma2, nobody gonna be hurtin' Kate and Essie Lou anymore, is they?"

Momma2 didn't answer right away. She put her hands down on the table and looked over ta me. "I wish I could answer "no," but that isn't a truth, and I don't lie ta ya. I think trouble is gonna be comin' ta 'em, and we's gonna be in the middle of it. We stand for what we love, Tilly, so we'll try our best to make 'em safe."

Chapter 14

It was the middle of the afternoon when Doc Gibbs came back to check on Kate, and Sheriff Joe Taylor was with him. I got nervous when I seen 'em come up to the door. First time the law had ever been ta our house. They knocked, and Momma2 went to the door to let 'em in.

Sheriff Taylor took off his hat and let his ol' bald head air out. There was a sweat ring 'round his hat that made me think of the blood in Kate's hair—wet and dark. He nodded to Momma2 and held out his hand. Momma2 took it and said the welcomes she usually said to people come to visit us, which wasn't many.

"Lila, I'm goin' in to see how Kate is doin' while you talk with Sheriff Taylor." Doc Gibbs talked to Momma2 like he was bossin' her around. "I filled him in on a few things he needed to know, but he's gonna need you to fill in the rest. Y'all excuse me."

Doc Gibbs left the room. I watched him head back to Momma2's bedroom with his doctorin' bag. Essie Lou was in there with Kate.

Momma2 told Sheriff Taylor to go on out ta the porch whilst she got him a glass a sweet tea. When he went out, she told me to tend to my own business whilst she was talkin' to him. When she got the tea and went out to the porch, I sat with my back to the screen door and listened 'cuz I figured this was my business being's as it was maybe gonna be trouble for us.

Sheriff Joe Taylor was the one started with talkin'. "Lila, I got the Putter boys down to the jail. They's probably not gonna stay there long. What they tell me doesn't give me reason to let 'em go, but if'n the town gets wind of the story, more'n likely they's gonna have the town on theys side. You know the law, Lila. The girls done commited a crime 'gainst nature, and one of 'ems pregnant, and she ain't married. Ain't no one in these parts gonna cotton to 'em havin' a baby together, let alone raisin' it for they own. Ain't no body, 'cludin' me. Ain't normal, them girls. I gots the law on my side on this, Lila. The boys, they sure 'nuf done a bad thing, and I reckon a time in jail will be 'nuf for folks to forgive 'em for what they done. When the doc gets that girl fixed up, then I reckon I have to deal with the two of 'em then. 'Till that time, I s'posin they just fine here."

Momma2 hadn't said a word, and I couldn't see if'n her face was listenin' to what the sherriff was sayin', but I was, and it wasn't soundin' any part a right to me. What he was sayin' was all wrong. It was like he was sayin' Kate and Essie Lou done something worst than what Remi and Ronnie done to 'em and there was no part of right to that. I didn't move a muscle on account a I didn't want Momma2 findin' out I was in a listenin' place.

The sheriff started on talkin' again. "Lila, you listenin' ta me? Man's gotta do what a man's gotta do. Ain't no changin' what's been done. Gotta do what's right with what's happenin' here. I'm hopin' ya see where I am with all this."

I heard feet shuffle, and I was scared a gettin' found out, so I started to stand up and scoot off when I heard Momma2 take one a her big breaths. I knew the words that followed that breath was gonna be comin' out of her deep place.

"Sheriff, I reckon I do understand where y'all are coming from." Momma2's voice was real soft and low. I had to keep my ears real clear to make out ever' word she was sayin'.

"You made yourself plain as day. You thinkin' them two boys did your good work for ya, makin' them girls pay for what your nasty ol' mind thinks. Well, Sheriff," Momma2 said with a growl, "We're not ever gonna think the same on that. Those two boys need to be put away for all their days fer what they did to Kate and Essie Lou. No twistin' words to know what's wrong and what those two boys did was wrong. Tying up Essie Lou and then makin' her watch 'em beat Kate near to death; pushing an ol' broom handle in her to make them feel like they was real men. Now, they's nothin' right about that, and I'm not thinkin' like you think and never will.

"Now, this here's my land. Poe and me paid for it all by ourselves. Ain't never asked anything from the law, and I'm 'spectin' I don't see no need for the law now. Soon as Doc Gibbs gets done lookin' after Kate, the two a you better be scootin' on down the road. **You do know how ta find your way back, don't ya?**" Momma2 drug those words out like she was talkin' to Junie Bird. "I'm just askin', 'cuz you don't sound like ya got a lick a good sense in your head thinkin' lovin someone is worse than tryin' to kill someone. Just makin' sure on how your head is thinkin'. She took a deeper breath 'fore she finished her sentence. " If'n you'll excuse me, Sheriff, I got a family that's needin' me to help 'em and I don't have time to sit and listen to anymore of your bullshit."

Momma2 said a bad word. A real one. I could hardly breathe myself when I heard that word come right out a her mouth. "Tilly," I heard her say, "you best be gettin' outside to finish up your chores. Don't be sittin' there by that screen door all day. We got work to do."

I got up from my sittin' and started for the back door. I saw Doc Gibbs comin' out a Momma2's bedroom as I was walkin' there. His hands was holdin' on to the ol' brown doctor bag he carried with him all the time. When he saw Momma2, he stopped. Momma2 started talkin' even for he got a word out. "No need ya comin' back here, Doc. I'm givin' ya money to cover what ya done and that's all I'm gonna be askin' ya to do for us."

Momma2 went over to the mason jar she kept under the sink. It held her cash money and I saw her pull out some of the bills she'd saved. She walked back over to Doc Gibbs and handed it to him. "Doc Gibbs, you helped my family over the years and I'm grateful fer your help. We have to part ways now, and I'm askin' you and the sheriff to be respectful of me and my family and keep y'all story off the streets of Siloam Springs. If'n I get wind that anyone's aimin' to step on my land to hurt any of my family, and that includes Kate and Essie Lou—they's family; if'n ya'll feel that'd be necessary, I'll be ready with Poe's shotgun. I don't ask for trouble and I never cause trouble, but I can meet it if'n it comes my way. I s'pose you understand me."

Doc Gibbs didn't put out his hand to take the money, so Momma2 put the money on Doc Gibb's brown bag and started toward her bedroom. Momma2 turned around and finished what she wanted to say. "That there money will cover the time Tilly was sick and you comin' to help Kate. We'll just keep the apples we was plannin' to give ya. Doesn't seem y'all would want apples from people who think like us." She opened the door to her bedroom, walked inside, and closed the door.

I saw Doc Gibbs pick up the money and put it in his shirt pocket. He wiped at his brow with the back of his hand and walked to the porch. Sheriff Joe Taylor was there with his ol' sweaty hat on. I watched both of 'em walk out the door to the sheriff car they come in. I heard the car drive off, and when I went to the kitchen window, I could see the dust from it disappear down the road.

Instead of goin' outside to finish my chores, I tiptoed over to Momma2's bedroom door and opened it to peek in. She and Essie Lou was givin' Kate a sip a water, lifting her head real gentle as they did it. "Get in here and shut the door, Tilly." Momma2 said and nodded her head like it was okay to be there. "Don't need to be sneakin' 'round trying to hear and see what's goin' on. We don't have no need for secrets in this house."

She laid Kate's head down real careful on the pillow, then she looked over to Essie Lou. "Essie Lou, you got a family here. We're not your kin, but we're your family, same as. We're gonna get Kate fixed up, and when that baby of your'n comes along, we're gonna be here to make it welcome to this earth. But you got a job to do now, girl. You got to eat, sleep, and take care a yourself, so's that little thing you carryin' 'round inside yourself gets big 'nuf to be ready when it's time. I'm gonna be with Kate, now. I want Tilly to help you get some water boiled, and I want you to sit in the copper kettle and take a good soak. She'll go down to the slave house with ya for some clean clothes. You can sleep in my bed with Kate after you get cleaned up and have a bite to eat. Get goin'. You listen to what I say, and you do it without no business. We gonna take care of y'all."

Essie Lou took Momma2's hand then wiped away the tears that were run-nin' down her face. She leaned over to Kate and gave her a little kiss on her cheek then she looked over ta me. "Tilly, don't ever know what I'd do without cha, little girl. I'm needin' your sweet help."

I took Essie Lou's hand, and we walked out the door of Momma2's room. When Junie Bird saw Essie Lou, she put down her sewin' and looked at her. She saw my hand in Essie Lou's and she waved us away, like she knew we had business, but I knew she just didn't know no better. She was dumb when life stuff was goin' on. When Essie Lou started to go over to talk with Junie Bird, I pulled her my way. "Don't be messin' with her now, Essie Lou, you got busi-ness to do and we gotta get it done. Let's not be getting' Junie Bird stirred up." Essie Lou looked down at me and started for the back door. We heard Junie Bird hummin' away as we walked to the slave house to follow Momma2's orders.

We spent the rest of the day doing little things here and there. After Essie Lou had her a good soakin', she put on her clean clothes and went to lay down with Kate. Momma2 was in the bedroom fixin' Kate's bed so's it was comfortable and ready for Essie Lou. When Essie Lou come back in and lay down, Momma2 brought out one of Junie Bird's quilts and put it over her. I saw her pet on Essie Lou's head 'fore she left the room and let her sleep. When I walked out a Momma2's bedroom, Momma2 took her hand and put it on my shoulder. "Tilly," she said, " You are the best thing come out of a sad happenin', and they's gonna be good come out a this. We's just gonna have to be strong whilts it's gettin' there. I got some chores to do while the girls are sleepin'. I'm s'posin' you do too. Let's get 'em done."

Essie Lou slept most of the afternoon with Kate. When she got up she quilted some with Junie Bird, and continued to helped Momma2 with Kate. She didn't want to be too far away from Kate.

After work, Zeke come over for dinner, but first he went into Momma2's room to see Kate. He took his time in there, and when he come out, his eyes had water in 'em. He wiped the water away with the hankies Essie Lou had made him. Essie Lou went over to him and gave him a hug, "Mr. Zeke, thank ye fer helpin' us. We's can never thank ya 'nuf for all you done. When Kate gets better she'll work extra hard to make it up to ya. That's a fer shore thing."

"Miss Essie, you's don't owes Zeke nothin' fer nothin'. Ol' Zeke's just sorry he didn't hear those ol' boys down to the slave house workin' on ya and hur-tin' ya, I's sorry more'n words that they could hurt y'all."

Essie Lou put her hand on Zeke's arm. "Ain't nothing ya coulda done to stop 'em from doin' what they did. They had that in they's head to do, and they was gonna get it done one way or the other. We all gonna just get better and go on."

Momma2 called us to the dinner table. Junie Bird was already sittin' there waitin' for her food. She still didn't know nothin' 'bout what happen ta Kate and Essie Lou. She had her hands on the table weavin' her fingers 'round the air like they was playin' on a string. Her mind was in a place all its own; that was fer sure.

When Essie Lou sat down by Zeke, Momma2 started talkin'. "Zeke, we's gonna be needin' a darkie doctor to look after Kate. I'm 'suposin' you know a midwife could take care a Essie Lou when her time comes on. Can you ask the darkie's workin' fer ya to find us some help for the girls?"

Zeke looked up from his dinner plate, "Yes'm, Miss Lila. We's gonna find someone."

That was it. Nothing else was said 'bout it, and sure 'nuf, the next night a darkie doctor shows up at our house to see Kate 'long with a woman name a Ma Bess. His name was Doc Samson. Doc Samson and Ma Bess come to the door with Zeke. Zeke don't have to knock to come inside, so he just come in and tell Momma2 they names.

"Miss Lila, this here's the docta gonna help out Kate and Essie Lou. Ma Bess, she helps when she needs. They's both a 'em gonna make shure every-thin' gonna turn out good."

"Right nice to meet y'all" Momma2 said with her hand held out ta shake. The doctor took her hand and gave it a shake, and Ma Bess put her hand on top a Momma2's hand and patted it like a handshake that meant somethin' more than regular, like she was talkin' with that pat.

"I'll show you on in to Kate and Essie Lou. You give 'em the time ya need and if'n y'all need somethin', y'all just call me to help ya. Zeke, I 'preciate ya findin' us help."

Momma2 turned to thank Zeke with her head nod, but he was already goin' out the door to his lean-to. He musta spent his after work dinner time gettin' the doctor and Ma Bess 'cuz he didn't come to eat with us."

Momma2 turned to lead the doctor and Ma Bess to her bedroom. I stayed put, on account a it was doctorin' business and I knew better. When they come out of the room, 'bout an hour later, Momma2 was smilin' and so was Ma Bess. No tellin' why that was, but it felt like it was a good thing to be doin' smilin', like they was.

Ma Bess was a skinny woman with shiny black skin and gray streaked hair that had a mind a its own. It was wiry and wild. Her eyes had a sparkle to 'em that made ya feel like she could be happy even when things might not be so good. I liked how the room felt with her in it. She had a flour sack dress on and I knew that 'cuz Momma2's flour came in the same material and we had tea towels looked just like her dress. She had big brown boots on her feet for shoes. I could tell they was too big fer her feet, but she didn't seem to care any. Just kept walkin' in 'em.

Doc Samson was a little man, not like the name he was named for. He was tiny and made Momma2 look like she was big, which she wasn't. His hands, though, was big. They looked like they was made for wrappin' 'round trees. His fingers was long and strong lookin', and his brown doctorin' bag looked like his fingers was too big to hold it.

"Can I get y'all some pie for ya have to go on home? I made some the other day with some mulberries I picked from the tree out yonder. I'd cut ya a slice if'n you would want a piece."

Ma Bess shook her head and so did the doctor. "No, thank ya, Ma'am. We's be goin' off for the night." The doctor talked, and Ma Bess just nodded her head like he was usin' the words she was thinkin'. "Miss Kate done been hurt something awful, but she'll mend in time. I be wantin' ya to put them cold presses on her to keep the swellin' down. Time take for the bruise color to go 'way, but time be a hard thing to take the scare out a her. Zeke done told me 'bout the pole stuck up in her. She gonna have some trouble with that for a good spell, but I's put a jar a medicine by your bed. You spread that 'round her bottom twice each day and make sure it don't turn red. If'n you see any red, you tell Zeke come get me right off. Ma Bess be with Essie Lou when her time comes. No one better at helpin' with woman time than she is."

Ma Bess smiled when he said that. I saw a bunch of her bottom teeth was missin'. Didn't hurt her smile none 'cuz it just opened wide and let the air go through her mouth big as day.

Momma2 walked outside with both of 'em and I saw her hug Ma Bess 'fore she got in the car with Doc Samson. Momma2 seemed to be huggin' lots more than her normal self.

I watched from the screen door. Junie Bird was in the corner hummin', Kate and Essie Lou was in Momma2's bedroom gettin' better, Zeke was in his lean-to probably eatin' a can of beans for his supper, and Momma2 was walkin' back to the house like nothin' in the world was different. But it was. I knew it even if'n I was only seven years old. I just didn't know what the different was gonna be.

Chapter 15

The sun was shinin' down, and Kate was sittin' up in a chair outside under the porch roof with a light quilt over her legs. Her skin was still a little yella lookin', but the blue and black spots that was there the night the Putter twins hurt her was goin' away. Her nose was lookin' like a nose though it had a curve in it at the top that couldn't be hid, and her mouth was regular sized with her lips lookin' like Kate's lips, soft and red. There was one scar near her right eye—didn't look like it would go away. A way to remember that awful night.

Even though Kate had been hurt something terrible, she could still talk. I mean, the accident didn't make her turn quiet like Essie Lou when she had the bad accident that made the baby in her belly. Kate's words was quiet, but they was still words.

Essie Lou's baby was growin' right big and there was nothing stoppin' me knowin' she was gonna be a momma 'fore too long. She could hardly bend over to pick up material to sew on. She had her quilt pieces on her fat lap, sewin' and talkin' real quiet like to Kate.

Life was still goin' on, kinda normal like. Junie Bird was still inside the house sewin' her quilt in the rocker by the winda. She had been workin' on a big quilt and it was takin' up most of the quiltin' frame. She had her head bent over the frame with the needle goin' in and out. The in and out movement was steady and her stitches was straight. Junie Bird shore'nuf was a marvel at her quiltin', even if'n she couldn't think a lick.

I could hear the orchard buzzin' with all the work that was bein' done to get the apples ready to get off the trees soon.

The Putter twins was out a jail. Like the sheriff said, they wasn't gonna be in too much trouble for what they did 'on account a what people thought of Kate and Essie Lou. Some people even thought them dumb ass crackers did the right thing.

But, last Saturday, when Momma2, Zeke, and me went in to Siloam Springs, Mrs. Malcolm and her girls was in the general store gettin' some more new material. Seemed like they was always buyin' up material to make themselves somethin' new to show off. Mrs. Malcolm whispered somethin' under her breath 'bout Momma2. Momma2 heard her and so did I. She said real quiet like, "Well, well, well, if it's not Miss Lila. Wonder if she's here buying something special for one of her girls?"

She drug the word girls out a her mouth like it was somethin' nasty. I looked at her with my eyes real narrow and was 'bout to sayin' something right back to her when I felt Momma2's hand on my shoulder. I saw Momma2 turn to Mrs. Malcolm and look her right in the eyes. She moved real close to her like she was gonna touch her, but she didn't. She just put her face real close to Mrs. Malcolm's face and said real friendly like , "Well, yes, ma'am, I reckon I'm here for the same reason you are. We have family we need to take care of, and we're doin' it just like we always do. Isn't that right, Tilly? We're just takin' care of our business and not hidin' nothin' from nobody, lest of all anybody with a nose so big it stuck in ever'body's business."

After Momma2 said that, she turned to Mr. Tribble. "You can go ahead and ring us up now—we'll be done for today. It's gettin' a bit too stuffy in this buildin' for me."

Mr. Tribble bent his head real low and I think I saw a smile on his face, but I couldn't put a bet on that. He rang Momma2's bill up then handed it to her. We had a runnin' credit in the store, and when the apples got sold off, then Momma2 came in and paid the bill full up. She took the credit bill in her hands, folded it up, and turned to Mrs. Malcolm. "You have a real nice day now."

Mrs. Malcolm had a red in her face that powder couldn't hide. She put her hands on her girls' shoulders, turned them around, and marched off to a different part of the store. Momma2 took my shoulder and steered me to the door. When we got out, Zeke had loaded all the supplies and was in the truck waitin' for us. Momma2 had left Junie Bird with Kate and Essie Lou back to the house so it was just us three in the front of the truck. When we got going down the road, Momma2 spoke over to Zeke. "Nothin' gonna stop people from thinkin' what they thinkin' 'bout those two girls, Zeke. I don't want ya to have any trouble in your life, so if'n ya need to move to a different place, you know I understand."

I couldn't believe my ears. Momma2 talkin' 'bout Zeke goin' to some other place. What in hell's name was she thinkin'? He was *our* Zeke. He couldn't leave us. What would we do without him? I looked over to Zeke and was about to tell him Momma2 wasn't thinkin' right and he shouldn't listen to her, but he put his hand on my knee and started his words first. "Zeke ain't gonna be goin' anywhere, Miss Lila, 'ceptin right where he's been for the last twenty-seven years. You gonna plant me next to my Belva and baby girl. Ol' Zeke, he ain't never gonna be leavin yous. You don't be talkin like that anymore."

He patted my knee with two pats like that was the end of the conversation and I guess it was 'cuz they didn't say no more words after that. Momma2 stared out the winda with her hands on the wheel, lookin' straight ahead. The wind was blowin' her hair away from her face. Zeke turned his head to look out the winda', and he didn't turn it back until Momma2 stopped the truck.

Momma2 and me took the supplies we bought inta the house while Zeke picked up the box he needed for the barn and headed that way. When we got inside, she put the bags in the kitchen and then went over to Junie Bird and handed her a stick a peppermint. Junie Bird put her needle and thread down to put that stick in her mouth like it was some kind of wonderful. She rocked back and forth while she sucked on that stick. I could see her lips turnin' red from the color.

Momma2 took two more peppermint sticks out to Kate and Essie Lou and handed one to me. Kate and Essie Lou was both full of thank y'alls, and when Momma2 sat down, Kate asked her how the trip was.

Momma2 didn't tell Kate that Mrs. Malcolm caused her ta get her dander up. She just said we got ever'thing we done needed for the week and we was set.

I watched Kate's bruised eyes look to Momma2 and then me. I think she was tryin' to see what Momma2 wasn't sayin', but Momma2 just kept her story to herself.

The followin' week when Momma2 was getting' ready to go to town, she told me it was best I stayed home with Kate and Essie Lou.

I wasn't gonna go with that decision without speakin' my mind about it. I spoke up loud and clear, "Momma2, why I's gotta stay home with Kate and Essie Lou?"

I left Junie Bird out of the question 'cuz she would be stayin' home being watched by Kate and Essie Lou, too. "I won't cause you no trouble, and I can help you and Zeke with the gettin'."

Momma2 looked over to me. "Tilly, you remember my talk with ya. I don't want you mixed up with any trouble, and I want you here to help with things. Essie Lou's gettin' close on to her time for that baby to be born, and she might need ya to help her with Kate. I'm countin' on ya to be a helpin' hand to those two girls if'n they need anything. You got two good legs on ya, and ya got a good head on your shoulders, so I'm leavin' ya here to be a help. You think that you can do that for me?"

I listened to Momma2's talkin' and, by the time she finished with her words, I felt she was makin' me in charge of the whole place whilst she and Zeke was gone. Made me feel pretty big for sure. "Sure, Momma2, I can do that for ya. I'll do what they need me to do while you and Zeke go to town."

Zeke and Momma2 piled into the truck—Momma2 drivin' like she always done and Zeke hangin' his elbow on the windowsill of his open window. I watched the truck head down the road. Dust a flyin'.

I spent the mornin' sittin' with Kate and Essie Lou in the back yard. Kate just sat there with the sun comin' down on her like water from the spring.

She held her head back to catch the sunshine on her face. I looked at her for a while and could see the shadows of the bruises still holdin' on. I had to turn away when I saw those, rememberin' the night those damn Putter twins beat on Kate for lovin' Essie Lou.

Essie Lou heard the car come up the driveway 'fore any of the rest of us. She was scared. I could see that right off. Kate was still weak and couldn't move very fast, and Essie Lou was big and fat with the baby growin' inside a her, so it was up to me to go see who was comin' to see us. I told Essie Lou and Kate I'd run see who come see us and for 'em to just wait here. I took off around the house and when I got to the front, I could see Sheriff Joe Taylor and one a his deputies gettin' out a their car. I could see their badges from where I was. I stopped in my tracks wonderin' if'n I should go talk to 'em. Sheriff Joe Taylor saw me and called out, "Hey, there, Tilly, go get your grandma fer me. I need to talk to her and those two girls livin' with y'all."

I knew Momma2 was my grandma and Junie Bird was my momma, but nobody ever used the word grandma around here, so it sounded like he was askin' me to go get someone I didn't know. I just stood there starin' and not movin'.

"Did y'all hear what I said, Tilly? Go get your grandma. I got words with her! Now do what I told ya!"

Sheriff Joe Taylor didn't sound so friendly the second time he told me to go get Momma2. "She isn't here, Sheriff Taylor. She and Zeke done gone off for supplies for the week. She be home around noontime, I s'pect."

"We's here to talk to those two girls livin' on your place. Where they at, now?"

Something inside my stomach started to turn over and make me feel sick. I didn't want to stop the law, but my stomach knew I needed to make Kate and Essie Lou safe, and the sheriff didn't feel safe.

"Sir, they's pretty sick and can't see no company right now." I said it with a soft voice, but it was shakin' a bit when I said it.

Sheriff Joe Taylor started walkin' toward me, talkin' while he did. I stepped away from him on account of I didn't like him close to me, "We can talk with 'em when they's sick. I don't think what they got is catchin' any. You just tell me where they are now."

I could see the sheriff's jaw get all tight, and his eyes narrowed down so they was lookin' at me real mean. I lifted my finger real slow and pointed to the back of the house. The sheriff and his deputy started back. I could feel the sweat on me rollin' down my face worried for Kate and Essie Lou. I followed behind the two men, my head down as I walked. When we came 'round the back of the house, Kate and Essie Lou was gone. I couldn't for the life of me know how they disappeared, but they was gone and I didn't know where they was.

Sheriff Joe Taylor turned sharp to me and with his eyes real narrow said, "You foolin' with me, girl? I don't have time fer yer nonsense. I come to talk with the girls and I mean to talk with 'em. Now, where are they?"

I put my hands up in the air like I'd made someone disappear. "Sir, I don't rightly know where they done gone off to. They been mighty sick. Maybe they be walkin' in the woods down by the creek, gettin' 'way from this here heat. It been right hot, isn't it?" I asked him a question tryin' to stay off his skinny eyes lookin ' at me.

He spit some tobacca out of his mouth and it landed near my foot. It was dark brown and slimmy lookin' and it had a stink to it that came up to my nose. "We's gonna look 'round this place fer a bit. You stay put!"

The sheriff and his deputy took off toward the slave house, and I figured they'd be findin' Kate and Essie Lou there and make themselves a worry to both of 'em, but a few minutes later they was back and I knew they hadn't found 'em there. They headed for the barn, then when they come back, they went right inside a Momma2's house like it was their own. They didn't even tell me they was goin' inside of our house. Marched right in with no knockin'.

While they was inside, I kept lookin' around to see if I could see where Kate and Essie Lou went off to, but I couldn't see 'em anywhere. I was stayin' put, just like the sheriff told me, but I wasn't likin' it any. That big glob of tobacca was right near my foot and ever' once in a while my eyes would catch a look at it and it made my stomach want to be sick.

They was 'bout to get my dander up with 'em being so nosy and goin' into places they wasn't invited in. I was holdin' my breath for fear they'd find the girls inside, but when I heard 'em askin' Junie Bird where was Kate and

Essie Lou, I knew the girls had disappeared into someplace I didn't know. Junie Bird started her loud hummin' and kept it up even when they asked her over again where was the girls. She just hummed louder and louder, until they finally give up on her. When they come back outside, I could see red in Sheriff Joe Taylor's face. He talked straight to me like I was older than I was.

"Listen to me straight on, Tilly. I mean to talk to those two girls and nothin' gonna be stoppin' me. They may be gone off now, but I'll be back, and when I come back, I 'spect to see 'em here. They's red car is over there, so I know they be 'round here somewhere. You tell your grandma I be back."

Sheriff Joe Taylor turned to his deputy, "Let's get goin'. We'll get them dykes the next time we be out this way. They ain't goin' nowhere with one of 'em pregnant and the other with the shit beat out a her." I could hear the mean in his voice as I listened to him talk to his deputy.

They both got in the car. The sheriff made a lot a dust when he turned the car and peeled out of our driveway. Seemed like he was yellin' at me with his car. When they was way down the road, I hurried to the back of the house. The two chairs was there and Essie Lou's quiltin' was on the chair, but they was for sure gone. I screamed their names over and over as I ran 'round outside between our house and the slave house. When I was comin' up to our house the second time, I thought of the root cellar. It was down behind the house behind some ol' huckleberry bushes and, unless you knew where it was, you wouldn't know it was there. I ran over to it and tried hard to open the door. I pulled and tugged at it, but my skinny ol' arms couldn't make it come up. I started cryin' tryin' to get it. I cried out for Kate and Essie Lou and pretty soon I felt the door push open and saw both of their eyes lookin' up at me from that dark hole in the ground. I cried even harder when I seen 'em.

With Kate pushin' with all her hurt self and me pullin' for all my seven years, we got the door open and they climbed out. Kate was slow movin', and still walkin' like her bottom hurt. Essie Lou was carrin' that big belly of hers, so she was even slower than Kate. When they got to the top of the stairs, we all hugged ourselves together, and that's when I saw they was cryin' too.

I didn't know how they knew they should hide, but I was glad they was smart and hid. No tellin' what that ol' sheriff had in mind, and he had a deputy to help him do it if'n he had a mind to.

Kate and Essie Lou patted my back and told me it was goin' be okay. They was talkin' like it was me the sheriff was havin a conniption about. They was tryin' their best to make me feel safe. I knew then that I loved them two girls like they was my own family. I knew I never wanted anybody to hurt 'em, and I was goin' to fight to make sure nobody did.

We all walked over to the chairs where Kate and Essie Lou sat down. Essie Lou asked if I needed some water from the pump. I shook my head no. She went over to the pump and pumped water on her hands, then held the water to her lips and drank. After that, she carried water over to Kate in the dipper that hung by the pump. Kate held the water with her lips and let it go slow down her throat. Essie Lou put her hand to Kate's head and wiped water over it to make her cool. Kate's eyes closed for a minute and when she opened 'em, she talked to me real slow. "Tilly, it's best Essie Lou and me go on down to our house and gather up our stuff. I'm not as strong as I need to be, so could I ask you to help us put our things in the car?"

"What cha meanin' to do, Kate?" I asked her straight in her face, so she couldn't be hidin' anything from me. "You and Essie Lou goin' someplace?"

I was standin' by Kate and Essie Lou was standin' right behind her. Kate took my hand and put it in her hand real tight. "Tilly, it's best we go now."

I could see Essie Lou's eyes fill with tears. They was runnin' down her face like pump water outa the pump. Kate's voice was chokin' and I could see she was wantin' to cry just like Essie Lou. She got up from the chair real slow. She and Essie Lou started down to the slave house. I'm thinkin' they woulda' been long gone 'fore Momma2 and Zeke got back, but 'bout half way down to the slave house, I heard Essie Lou make a loud noise and saw her bend over like a snake had bit her. I run to see what happened.

Kate had worry spread 'cross her face, like the sheriff had come back. I started to cry again and this time I didn't even know why. Essie Lou's body was bent over in pain and she was cryin' out to Kate. Kate could hardly bend over 'cuz her bottom was still a hurtin. Essie Lou raised her head in the air makin' her cry ring through the trees and fill the air. She was down on her knees now holdin' her fat belly with both a her hands and rockin' back and forth tryin' to get away from the pain. It held on!

"It's the baby, Kate!" I heard her say between her screams. "Oh my God, it's the baby!"

Kate slowly got down to be with Essie Lou. They was both on the ground. Kate had Essie Lou's head and was lookin' her direct in the eyes. She talked real slow to her like she was Junie Bird. "Listen here to me, Essie Lou. I'm right here. I'm right here beside you."

The pain musta left Essie Lou for a minute 'cuz she stopped her screamin' and looked right to Kate. Sweat was runnin down her red face. Her eyes didn't leave Kate's face. Kate kept on talkin'. "Shh, there now, Essie, we need to get you to bed. Can you stand up and walk?"

Kate took hold a Essie Lou's hands and talked real slow and quiet to her. Essie Lou looked like she was more scared than the night the Putter twins snuck in and hurt 'em. She took a deep breath and tried to stand. Kate brought her body up to standin' right along Essie Lou. Essie Lou started walkin' to the slave house, takin' real slow steps. Kate walked right beside her holdin' on to her arm as they walked. I kept my steps right even with theirs.

I looked at the Eve tree as we walked by it. It stood there. It had been part of something so awful to Kate and Essie Lou. The leaves hung down and twisted 'round like they was ashamed of what they was a part a.

My swing was torn down. The Putter twins had used its rope to tie up Essie Lou and make her watch them hurt Kate. Other pieces of the rope had been wrapped 'round Kate whilst they did awful things to her. I put my eyes down as I walked by it. I didn't see Kate or Essie Lou look at the tree as they walked by it. I didn't know how they could.

While we walked, I could hear Essie Lou's low groanin', but she wasn't screamin' anymore. She and Kate just kept up theys steady walkin', and so did I. When we got to the slave house, Essie Lou stopped and took a deep breath 'fore she put her foot on the step to go up to the house. Kate stopped with her. "We're almost there, sweet girl. You're almost there. Just a little bit further and you can rest."

Kate rubbed Essie Lou's arms and kissed her cheek. Essie Lou put her hand on top of Kate's then raisin' her foot continued up the steps into the slave house. When she got to their bed, she sat down and Kate helped her put her feet on the bed. Kate took off Essie Lou's shoes and pulled up a chair to sit beside her.

"Tilly, go over to our ice box and get out a jug of water, then bring it to me for Essie Lou. Will you, please?"

I turned right fast and run for the jug. When I got back, I could see Essie Lou was fixin' to scream again. I was right worried Sheriff Joe Taylor would hear her and come drivin' back to get 'em. I handed Kate the water jug, then stood there while I watched Essie Lou's body take over the room with its hurtin'.

Kate held on to Essie Lou's hand. It looked like Essie Lou was gonna break Kate's hand from the holdin'. Essie Lou cried out. Her body twisted, and her eyes looked like they was beggin' us to help her, but I didn't know how and I don't think Kate did either. When her screamin' was over, her body fell back on the bed and Kate turned to me. "Tilly, you have to run to wait for Momma2 and Zeke. When they get here, you tell Zeke to run get Ma Bess. It's Essie Lou's time to have her baby. Go now. I'll take care of Essie Lou until you get back with Ma Bess."

I didn't wait for her to ask me again, I turned and run out of the slave house like a ghost was after me. I run to the front of our house and waited to see the truck. When I saw it, I started runnin' for it 'fore it even got to the house. Seemed like Zeke saw me comin' and Momma2 started drivin' fast to meet me. They pulled up and stopped. Momma2 jumped out a the truck and put her hands on my shoulders. "What is it, Tilly. What's wrong, girl?" Her eyes was wide open and I could feel the shakin' of her hands on my shoulders. Zeke was right beside me waitin' on me to talk.

It's Essie Lou down to the slave house, Momma2. She's done been scream-in and hurtin'. She needs Ma Bess right fast." I looked to Zeke then. "Zeke, Kate done asked me to tell ya to run get Ma Bess ta help Essie Lou get her baby born."

Zeke didn't wait for anything else. He jumped back in the truck and, 'fore I knew it, he was down the road with dust runnin' after him. Momma2 didn't wait fer me. She took off like a lightin' bug and left me in the road. When I seen her go past the red car headin' for the slave house, I took after her. I knew I had other things to tell her 'bout this day, but it was gonna have to wait.

Chapter 16

I was sleepin' on the porch of the slave house but was suddenly awakened to the sound of a baby's cry. It was a loud, firm cry that made me jump to my feet.

When Momma2 got to the slave house that afternoon, she ran right in to see what was goin' on with Essie Lou and Kate. I wasn't too far behind her. When I come through the door, I could see Kate sittin' in a chair next to Essie Lou lyin'in the bed. She had a rag of wet water and was coolin' Essie Lou's head and talkin' to her in a soft, quiet voice. Momma2 run to the bed. When Kate reached for her hand, Momma2 took it. Momma2 picked up the wet rag, poured some more water on it, and rung it out. She didn't pay no mind to the water she dripped on the floor—she just started wipin' down Essie Lou's face. I could tell Essie Lou was tired out from hidin' from the sheriff and, now, from that baby tryin' to come inta the world.

I'd watched the pigs and ol' Bossy's have their youngins. They made some animal sounds, they laid down on the ground, their eyes usually got all big and bulgy, but they never made no sounds like I heard Essie Lou make. Ever' time Essie Lou's screams came out, I thought she was fixin' to die. I near cried my eyes out with worry for her. Finally, Momma2 turned to me, "Tilly, this here's the way it is. It isn't easy gettin' into the world. That baby's fightin' to get out and breathe this good air of the earth, but it has to work hard to get here. This isn't gonna be easy for Essie Lou. You're not too young to know how life gets here, but I think it's best you stay out of here while we help Essie Lou. You go check on Junie Bird, wait for Ma Bess and Zeke, then wait out on the porch. If'n I need ya for anythin', I'll yell for ya.

I knew this was no time fer questions, so I did what Momma2 told me to do. When I got to the house, I went inside and looked at Junie Bird. She hadn't had anyone fix her lunch, so I poured her a glass a cold milk and made her a peanut butter and jelly sandwich. I used my favorite red jelly that Momma2 made from apples. Peanut butter and jelly sandwiches was what I made the best. When I called to Junie Bird, she put down her needle and walked over to the table. I never had a dog a my own, but I kinda figured Junie Bird came to the table like a dog woulda come to someone's call. She just did what she was taught to do and nothin' more. She didn't know anything was goin' on at the slave house, and I wasn't gonna tell her. Wouldn't be no use.

I watched her eat. She picked up her sandwich, ate a bite, then chewed that piece real slow. I think this was the first time I paid her eatin' any mind. She chewed like she sewed. She took her time. I was fixin' to tell her to finish her damn sandwich when I heard the truck pull up to the house. I ran out leavin' Junie Bird to takin' forever.

Zeke was already out of the truck and so was Ma Bess. She had a bag in her hand, and as little as she was, she carried that bag with her big hands, and it didn't seem to hold her down from runnin'. She took off like the wind, her big boots hittin' the ground with each step. I followed right behind.

As we come to the Eve tree, I could hear Essie Lou's screamin'. It made a place in my stomach go upside down. We all ran faster. Ma Bess went inside, but Zeke stayed outside on the porch with me. Havin' babies was a woman thing, and he wasn't gonna stick his nose where he knew better.

Sittin' there, I saw that Kate and Essie Lou had fixed up the porch real nice. They had chairs sittin' out and a bench with a back on it. Zeke sat in one a the chairs and I sat on the bench.

I musta fell asleep sometime on that bench while we was waitin'. It had been a long wait. Essie Lou cried and screamed. I could hear Momma2 and Ma Bess talkin' to her and rattlin' around in the house. I didn't know what they was doin', but whatever it was, I was hopin' it was gonna make that baby get here and stop hurtin' Essie Lou. Seemed like she and Kate had been hurt enuf. Then, all of a sudden a baby's cry woke me up!

A little while later, after I heard that cry, Momma2 come to the porch. She looked tired, and her hair was wet from sweatin'. She stood at the screen door fer a minute, then come over and sat down on the bench with me. She put her arm around my neck and bent down. I looked up at her, my eyes tired from the bench sleep.

"Tilly, Essie Lou done had her a baby boy. Zeke, I appreciate you bringin' Ma Bess to help us. She's fixin' Essie Lou and gettin' her set up with her new baby, then I reckon' she'll need ya to be takin' her back to her home. I need to go up to the house 'fore ya take Ma Bess on home to get her some cash money for the help she gave us. I 'll be wantin' her family to have some of our apples when the apples are ready. Zeke, you see that she gets 'em when the time comes. Make sure they are our best apples!"

Momma2 didn't say no more than that. I think she was tired, too, and was wishin' she could be in bed sleepin' away the work she had to do to help Essie Lou, but she patted me on the head, then walked up to the house to go get Ma Bess some cash money from her jar under the sink.

Zeke come over when she left and sat on the bench with me. "Well, Tilly girl, I be guessin' you's gonna have to be a big sister to that little fella, now. He's gonna be needin' ya and so's those girls."

Zeke put his arms around me and I laid my head right into his side. He patted my shoulder as he let me lean into him. We sat there like that 'til the screen door opened up and Ma Bess come out with her bag. She musta sweat somethin' fierce gettin' that baby boy out a Essie Lou 'cuz her skin was shinin' like our ol' copper tubs. She was smilin' to beat the band.

"Well, well, well, there chil', you done got youself a little boy chil' to bring up and play with, now. He gonna need his mamma for a good piece a time, but soon 'nuf he gonna be ready to play with. I 'magine you's gonna be the one to do that playin'. Miss Essie done a real good job bein' his mamma. She done real good."

I couldn't imagine Essie Lou being a momma. She was such a little thing, and her havin' a baby seemed a big jump for my mind to do. 'Sides that, her screamin' didn't seem like anythin' was good 'bout her becomin' a momma.

Ma Bess looked over to Zeke. Mr. Zeke, ya best be gettin' me home 'for the sun goes down. Don't want ya havin' no trouble 'cuz a me, now." She started up the trail as Zeke took his arm from 'round my shoulder and got up off the bench. I saw Momma2 meetin' Ma Bess on the trail, and knew she was handin' her over some cash money. Zeke looked down at me, and when he did, I thought of Sheriff Joe Taylor and his deputy and worried they might make trouble fer Zeke takin' Ma Bess home. "Zeke, why ya always gotta be back 'fore sundown. You don't do nothing wrong?"

Zeke looked down at me and tussled my already messed up hair. "Aw, Tilly girl, ol' Zeke, he bes scared a the dark, don't y'all know that?"

I didn't know that and I knew that wasn't the right answer, but I also knew that was the only answer he was gonna be givin' me, so I followed Zeke up to Momma2 and started tellin' her the Sheriff Joe Taylor story I been holdin' on to whilst Essie Lou was gettin' that baby out a her.

"Momma2, Sheriff Joe Taylor and some deputy I didn't know come here today to talk to ya and Kate and Essie Lou." I could see Zeke stop from takin' Ma Bess home and listen to my story. "That Sheriff Joe Taylor was real bossy and even walked in the slave house and our house without askin' permission. Kate and Essie Lou hid in the root cellar when he come. I didn't know they was scared a him, but they was. I could see scared on they faces when I found 'em. That sheriff even had Junie Bird hummin' like a crazy bird 'cuz he asked her questions she couldn't know. They sure shoulda knowed better than to ask her, but they pestered her anyway. They told me straight off they was comin' back to talk to the three a y'all and to tell ya so. I didn't tell ya 'fore on 'count a Essie Lou screamin' and hurtin' so bad."

I told the story straight through without one stop. Momma2, Zeke, and Ma Bess all stood straight there and listened to me. When I finally took a breath, Momma2 looked over to Zeke. "Zeke, you best stay here with the girls, and I'll take Ma Bess home, tonight. If'n ya need Poe's rifle, it's under my bed. It's ready for usin.'"

Then Momma2 looked at me. "Tilly, you did the right things, today. I don't want you and Junie Bird to be scared of anything. I'll be takin' care a this little visit from the sheriff. I reckon you and Zeke might just want to go see that new little boy Essie Lou worked so hard to get into this world. I'll fix y'all supper when I get back home. Junie Bird will be just fine 'til then."

Then Momma2 did the thing that made me wonder if'n she was goin' crazy like Junie Bird. She reached over and hugged me real tight. When she let me go, I could see her eyes lookin' over to Zeke. "I'll be back fast as I can, Zeke." Then she turned and her and Ma Bess headed up the trail leavin' us standin' there watchin' 'em.

"Well, Tilly girl, we's got us a little boy to go see, so let's get to goin.'" He put his hand on my shoulder to make sure I was headin' toward the slave house, and even though my feet wanted to follow Momma2, I followed Zeke.

When we got to the slave house, Zeke called through the screen door real quiet like.

"Miss Kate, Miss Essie, y'all okay if'n we come in?"

There was a rustle in the room, then we saw Kate at the door. Her eyes was smilin' even though they was tired. She opened the screen door. "Of course, come in, come in."

I was gettin' use to Kate talkin' like a Yankee. She just sounded like Kate to me, now. Zeke stepped inside a the door right behind me. The room was kinda dark 'cuz it was gettin' close to sunset. The whole day was gone from the sheriff comin' and the baby comin'. Essie Lou was layin' in the bed over on the other side a the room. A light was on, but it didn't show off a lot a shine. I could see Essie Lou was holdin' a blanket wrappin' up a baby. When I could see her face smile from the doorway, Zeke and I walked over real slow. Kate walked, too, but her walkin' was even slower than us. When we got to the bed, Essie Lou unfolded the blanket and there lay a little baby all red and puffed up. He had a head full a dark hair like Kate. His eyes was closed. I s'posed he was tired from all the work he had to do to get here. I heard Zeke, so I turned to see him. He was cryin' real tears and they was runnin' down his cheeks free from his eyes. I wasn't thinkin' there was any reason to cry, then I remembered his Belva and his baby girl, and thought maybe he was thinkin' Essie Lou and her baby might not be livin' much longer. As I reached for his hand, he grabbed on to mine and held it tight.

"Well, there, Miss Essie, you done did a fine job of makin' a son fer y'all. He gonna be a fine boy. Big and strong."

When Zeke said those words, I knew he wasn't worried. He was feelin' good, and the tears he was sheddin' was happy ones.

I never been 'round any babies, so I wasn't wantin' to touch it or anythin' like that. I just fixed my eyes on it and watched its hands twist in the air like it was feelin' where it was. I saw Essie Lou's eyes watchin' it, too. I could see the tired all over her face, but her face was full a happy. I was thinkin' she had to be real glad that baby was out a her belly and layin' on her lap.

Essie Lou folded the blanket 'round the baby, then held it up to Zeke. "I'd like ya to hold him if'n you want to, Zeke." She spoke real soft and quiet. Zeke's big, strong hands reached down to lift that little baby to his body and hugged it to him. The water from his eyes kept right on comin' down. Zeke didn't have any words when he was holdin' on to the baby. He just looked at it and then back to Essie Lou. The baby made a sound that made me think of the doves cooin' in the trees. Real bird like.

Zeke held on to the baby for a good long time, then he put the baby back in Essie Lou's arms. She looked over to me. "Tilly, he won't break none. If'n you want, you can come sit on the bed with me and touch him. He's real soft."

I went over to the bed to sit 'side a Essie Lou. The baby was still sleepin'. She opened up the blanket and guided my hand to his arm. I let my fingers glide over his skin up to his little fist. He held that fist tight like he was holdin' on to somethin' real important. As I touched his fist, his eyes fluttered open. They was lookin' right at me, and I could see he had eyes meant to look at the world, big and wide.

"Looky there, Tilly, he wants to say "hi" to y'all." Essie Lou smiled at me when she said that, makin' me feel a flutter inside my guts. I didn't know what that feelin' was, but it was good, and it felt like that all 'cuz a touchin' that baby. I was glad Essie Lou made him and he was here fer all a us. Zeke, too.

Kate had been standin' back a us watchin', and I saw Essie Lou look over to her. Neither of a 'em said anythin' 'bout 'em leavin' here like they was thinkin' this mornin'. I was hopin' that was out a their minds.

'Fore long, Zeke said, "Miss Essie and Miss Kate, Tilly girl and me gonna leave y'all ta rest with your young'un. Ain't long 'fore the sun be settin', and Miss Lila be back to get y'all some supper. We's gonna go to the house and see in on Miss Junie Bird."

"Thank you for comin' to see us," Essie Lou said first, then Kate said, "Tell Miss Lila we have food to eat tonight. Thank her for thinking of us and thank her for all the help she gave Essie Lou and our baby. We'll see you in the morning."

Kate walked us to the screen door and opened it for us. I turned to look at her to see if leavin' was in her eyes, but I couldn't see that. I didn't want to leave the porch on a'count a being scared they wouldn't stay. Kate reached over to me and put her arm on my shoulder. "Tilly, Essie Lou and me are real thankful for all you did for us today. You were real brave." With those words, Kate reached down and kissed the top of my head. It felt warm, and when our eyes come together, I could feel her lovin' me.

Zeke took my hand as we walked up the trail to the house. When we got to the Eve tree, Zeke stopped. He looked long and hard at it, and I felt for sure he was thinkin' 'bout Kate and Essie Lou being hurt. A big vein in the side a his head popped out and I could see his jaw get firm and stuck. I never seen that look on Zeke 'fore.

"Zeke, you be lookin at the Eve tree, and you be thinkin' on Kate and Essie Lou and them dumb crackers?"

Zeke was quiet for longer than was comfortable, but I didn't ask another question. I watched his eyes go up and down the tree. It's branches still held onto livin' and the green parts of it was full a life. The bark on the tree was heavy with moss, makin' it look like it was dressed up in forest colors, standin' there mindin' its own business. It was the biggest tree on our orchard but it didn't give off any fruit. It was just there for the pure beauty of it. That's what Momma2 use to say.

"Tilly girl," Zeke took a big breath 'fore he said any more, "Your Grandpa Poe and me dug the hole to plant that there Eve tree. He called her Eve, on account a she was the first. The hole was deep 'cuz them roots was bigger than the tree. Biggest roots I ever did see. I 'member the day us'en put it in the ground. We planted it good, and it done grown good. Yes'um, that tree done been through windstorms and tornadoes. Even had ice on it so heavy one year it done broke some of it's big ol' branches, but it still fightin' to live and it standin' good. Some things be planted fer the good they do, Tilly girl, and some things be planted fer bad. The Eve tree, she be planted ta do good, and she done good. I bettin' that ol' tree feel real sad she got used to be part a hurtin' Miss Kate and Miss Essie Lou. Them boys onliest ones to be part a the hurtin', and they be planted to do bad and they done it. Ol' Zeke don't want any more hurtin' done to them girls and they baby boy."

I could see the sad in Zeke as he held tighter to my hand. He used his other hand to put a pat on top of the hand he was holdin'. "We's gonna make sure Miss Kate and Miss Essie Lou and they's new little boy be safe as peas in a pod. We's gonna do that, Tilly girl. You, me, and Miss Lila. We's all gonna do that."

Seemed Zeke was done with his thinkin', so he started up the trail to the house leavin' the Eve tree and the slave house behind us. As we got up to the house, we could hear Momma2's truck coming down the road. We walked toward the truck to meet Momma2. When Momma2 stopped, she got out and looked over to both a us, "Zeke, Ma Bess is safe at home."

Zeke nodded his head when he heard that. He still had holda my hand, and we was all started walkin' toward the house.

"Miss Lila, Miss Kate said she done got some food to eat til tamorra." Zeke told Momma2, and she nodded, so he knew she heard.

"Best we go inside and get us some food on the table for all of us." Momma2 spoke as she walked. "Junie Bird will be needin' for us to be with her, and I reckon, tomorrow, I'll be goin' into town early to see the sheriff and make sure he knows we won't be needin' him to comin' visitin' to our place anymore."

Chapter 17

When I got up this mornin', Junie Bird was already sittin' at the breakfast table waitin' fer her breakfast and Momma2 was fixin' to sit down in front a her. Momma2 looked up when she saw me come out a my bedroom door. I was dressed fer the day when I noticed Momma2 had her Saturday clothes on, but it was Monday. So, 'course, I was wonderin' what the hec was goin' on.

"Junie Bird," Momma2 was talkin' at her even though Junie Bird was eatin' and not payin' one bit of attention to anything Momma2 was sayin'. She was just starin' at the wall on the other side a the kitchen like somebody was there. Junie Bird was like that. Always lookin' over at somethin' like there was somethin' there when there wasn't nothin'. I looked over to the wall just to make sure, but there was nothin' fer her to be starin' at. "Junie Bird," Momma2 said again to make Junie Bird's head turned to look at her. "I'm takin' the truck to town this mornin'. Tilly will be doin' her chores, and Kate and Essie Lou will be down to the slave house takin' care a their business. They got them a baby, Junie Bird. A little boy baby. He don't have a name yet, but I suppose, they'll figger one out for him for too long. When Essie Lou gets to feelin' better, she'll bring him up to say "hey" to ya. You just work on y'all's quilt while I'm gone. You stay in the house. Tilly will be watchin' for ya."

At that, Momma2 looked over to me and put her eyes straight on mine. "You heard what I told Junie Bird, Tilly. I'll be back 'for noon. You do your chores, and you take ta watchin' Junie Bird. Kate and Essie Lou might need y'all so go down to the slave house and check on 'em. I fixed extra biscuits this mornin' and there's some jam and milk. Take that down to the slave house when ya go. Don't be goin' off on your own this mornin'. I want ya to be close to the house just in case Junie Bird or Kate and Essie Lou need ya. I'm countin' on ya, Tilly."

Momma2 didn't look at me for a minute, so I thought out a question I needed ta ask 'fore she left. "What if Sheriff Joe Taylor and that deputy shows up to talk to y'all Momma2? He said he was fixin' to come back here."

I knew I shouldn't be scared a the law, but that Sheriff Joe Taylor left me feelin' scared for Kate and Essie Lou. I didn't want him scarin' 'em anymore, and I sure 'nuf didn't want him scarin' their new little baby boy.

"Don't you give no mind to the sheriff, Tilly. I'm gonna be drivin' to talk to him 'fore he can get in his car this mornin'. Get busy with your chores, now."

Momma2 took some cash money from the jar under the sink. I never seen her take cash money 'fore anythin' 'septin' to pay her big bill at the general store after apple time, but she took a wad of that money and pushed it down in her pocket.

Junie Bird finished her breakfast and got up to put her dishes in the sink. She learned that chore from 'fore I was born, and she was right good at it. No one ever had to clean up her dishes for her. Then she went to sit at her quiltin' frame. Momma2 walked over to her. "I'll be goin' Junie Bird. I'll be back for ya know it."

Junie Bird didn't even look up. She just started her hummin' and picked up her needle and thread. Momma2 nodded over to me, then left.

I did my inside chores a cleanin' my dishes then got the slop bucket and headed for the door. I got all my mornin' chores done quick as I ever did. When I got back to the house, Junie Bird hadn't moved from her sittin' place, so I gathered up the biscuits. Momma2 had wrapped 'em up in one a her kitchen towels made out a flour sack, then I grabbed the milk bottle sittin' by the sink. The bottle was cold, so I knew Momma2 had brought it in early this mornin'. I tucked the biscuits and the jam in one hand, put the milk bottle under my arm to hold it tight and headed out the door for the slave house.

As I walked down the trail, I could hear the tractor in the orchard gettin' fired up ready to go to work. I knew Zeke would be tellin' the workers what had to be done and where to get it done. I was glad them dumb Putter twins wasn't workin' on our orchard anymore. I was hopin' they was rottin' their asses in jail.

This was a busy time in the orchard on a'count a it being close to pickin' time. When pickin' time came on, the orchard would be buzzin' from sun-up to sundown and the barn would be loaded with apples and people. I was hopin' Kate was gonna get herself better, so'n she could get back to helpin' Zeke and not be thinkin' on leavin' here.

When I come up to the slave house, I could hear the baby cryin' and could hear the soft sounds of Kate and Essie Lou talkin' 'tween themselves. I set the milk bottle down and knocked real soft on the door screen. It wasn't long 'fore Kate opened it up. By then the baby was quiet.

"Well, there, good morning, Tilly. It's nice to see you so bright and early this morning."

Kate had a big smile on her face. She opened the door wide and swung the screen door open for me. I picked up the milk bottle and with the biscuits and jam in my hands, I walked inside.

Essie Lou was sittin' in a chair with that baby bundled up by her chest. She had a blanket over the top a her, and I could figur' she was givin' that baby some a her own milk. Essie Lou smiled over to me and gave me a wink with one a her big, brown eyes. "Good mornin' ta ya, Tilly. My little boy be eatin' him some breakfast. Soon as he's done, you can have another look at him if'n y'all want to." I didn't say nothin', just set the milk and biscuits down on the table and walked over to stand by Kate. Kate put her arm on my shoulder.

"Momma2 done left for town to talk to that Sheriff Joe Taylor and his deputy."

I could see Essie Lou's eyes look over to Kate, and I could tell they both was scared.

Kate took her hand down from my shoulder and went over to stand close to Essie Lou. They was lookin' at each other, and even though they wasn't sayin' no words, I knew they was wantin' to get away from hearin' about that sheriff. I felt somethin' awful for sayin' anything 'bout that ol' sheriff.

Essie Lou's eyes fell lookin' down to her baby. I stood there watchin' her. She pulled the sleeve of her dress up then lowered the blanket off'n her shoulder. There was that little baby layin' on her lap. His baby eyes was closed to ever'thing. Essie Lou sat lookin' at him for a good long time, and no one was talkin'. I was lookin' at him, too. He looked so new. He still had a little red on his face, and his black hair looked like a rug spread out all over his head. Essie Lou raised up her head from lookin' down and wiggled her finger to me to come closer; I did. When I got there by her chair, she looked up to my eyes. "Tilly, I reckon you ain't seen a baby this little 'fore now. He's gonna grow right big fast as you can count. I got me six little brothers and sisters and it don't take no time fer 'em to be big as can be. For ya know it, he's gonna be wantin' to play with ya." She smiled when she said that, and I smiled back hopin' she forgot about the sheriff.

"Tilly, if'n y'all want to, go sit on the bed, and I'll bring this little one over to lay on your lap fer a spell. You can't hurt him none."

That thought plumb froze me! I looked at her then lowered my eyes. "Thank y'all, Essie Lou fer offerin' your new baby to my lap, but I'm not thinkin' that there's a good idea fer me. I'll just touch on his arm, if'n you don't care."

With that, I put my finger on his little baby arm and run it up and down feelin' that soft baby skin and thinkin' on how Essie Lou done made him all by herself. She was a real good maker fer babies.

Kate offered me a biscuit and jam and milk, but I already done had my breakfast and didn't need no more. I petted on that baby's arm for a couple more times, and then told 'em if'n they didn't need me fer nothin', I was gonna go check on Junie Bird, which I did. I skipped all the way up to the house thinkin' 'bout that new baby.

I come through the back door and could hear Junie Bird's hummin' and knew she was quiltin'. I never did do no quiltin' myself on account of I never did learn how to do it. When I went up to see Junie Bird, I decided to sit by her and watch her move her needle where it needed to go. She kept her eyes to the material. The needle and thread seemed to follow a line her eyes musta made 'cuz it was straight as an arrow. She hummed her bird-like hum all the time she sewed.

As I sat watchin' her pass her time away, I thought all about Junie Bird makin' me. She had me in her belly same as Essie Lou had her baby boy. Then I thought on how Momma2 made Junie Bird. One of the jobs women had was makin' babies, and it was hard work doin' it. My mind was thinkin' I didn' much want that job.

I sat in the chair watchin' on Junie Bird fer most a the mornin'. I tried to read on my new library book, but my head kept goin' to Momma2 and the sheriff and those thoughts kept me from readin' any words. I kept waitin' fer the truck sound to come back up the road. I waited a long time. When my ears finally heard the sound of somethin' comin' up the road, I knew it weren't no truck. I run to the window to see who was comin' and wouldn't you believe it. It was that damn Sheriff Joe Taylor's car stirrin' up dust and soundin' like he was racin' to a fire. I run to the door and went outside. When I looked at that sheriff's car, I saw Sheriff Joe Taylor's deputy man sittin' in the car right 'side a him. They didn't get out a the car like I figer'ed they would. They just sit there. That puzzled my mind some, then I saw Momma2's truck come speedin' in and pull up right 'side of the sheriff. She jumped out of her truck and run right over to his car window and started talkin' right loud, like he was deaf or something was wrong with his ears.

"Joe, I come to your jail, this mornin' tryin' to talk sense into y'all. You thinkin' I'm just an old woman and I don't have no say about what happens on my land. You think you can boss me about who lives here and what they do? Well, you best be thinkin' again 'cuz there isn't anythin' I won't do to protect my family and my land. Poe's gun is over in that truck and it's loaded to use. I'm not wantin' to shoot y'all, but you cause any problems' for me or my people, you gonna have problems with me. You got that?"

I saw Sheriff Joe Taylor open his car door with a push. Momma2 moved out of the way of the door but held her ground. She started on talkin' to him again. This time she put her finger up like it was a stick and pointed it to his face.

"I never turned nobody away from my land. I even gave jobs to those two awful Putter boys who nearly killed my Kate and forced Essie Lou to watch 'em do it. And you let 'em out a your jail. How you could do that is way beyond my thinkin'. But you did it, and I can't stop that happenin'. You gotta be sick in the head to let 'em go free."

Momma2 was talkin' to the sheriff like she was his boss. And she left off the sheriff part of his name and just called him "Joe."

"Are you forgettin' all the time your pappy and your brother come here pickin' apples when you was a young'un? You played real nice with Junie Bird when she wasn't nothin' more than a crawler."

Momma2 stood a good foot shorter than Sheriff Joe Taylor, but she was talkin' loud and strong at him, makin' me think she felt a lot bigger than she was. She put down her finger and stared up to him. Her voice got softer, but it held on to her deep place.

"When your brother up and left town, Poe and me was real sad 'bout that, and we didn't put no weight on what people was sayin' 'bout him. Poe and me never done you anything but good. We was all friends. Good God in Heaven, where'd that Joe go? I need to know, on a'count of this Joe messin' with my business, isn't the Joe I use to know."

That's when Sheriff Joe Taylor put his hand in the air, like a signal for Momma2 to stop talkin' and she did.

"Best ya leave my brother out a this, Lila. This here is sheriff business, and I best get to doin' it without ya in the middle of it."

He started walkin' down the trail, then turned and pointed his finger at his deputy. "Get the hell outa the car, William. You ain't gettin' paid to sit on your ass."

The deputy hurried out of the car, fixin' his hat as he got out. He followed behind the sheriff, makin' sure his gun and holster was sittiin' right on his hip as he walked.

They walked to the red car and when they got there, they stopped. The sheriff pushed his hat back on his forehead, and I could see the bald part of his head shine out. "Them girls sure do have a fancy car for farm workers. Don't suppose they be wantin' to part with it do ya?"

"That car belongs to the girls. I don't rightly know if'n they be wantin' to part with it or not. That there's their business, not mine. I don't stick my nose in anybody's business that isn't mine to be in." She turned her head to look at me, and her eyes drilled into me like red hot coals in the stove.

"Tilly," Momma2 yelled over to me . "I can't seem to talk Sheriff Joe Taylor into mindin' his own business." She said his full sheriff name and made it sound like she thought it was bullshit to have a name like that.

"Seems he's bound and determined to go down to the slave house and bother your cousins. You go tell cousin Kate and cousin Essie Lou the sheriff and his deputy be down to see 'em in a few minutes. You make sure they are dressed and ready to meet him and this here deputy of his. You make sure your cousins be ready fer him."

Momma2 said the word cousin four times to make sure I heard her good. I never heard Momma2 lie before and to hear her talk 'bout Kate and Essie Lou being cousins near sent me in a tailspin. I knew better than say somethin' 'bout tellin' the truth, so I run like the wind down to the slave house. I didn't even knock on the door. I just run inside, my heart beatin' nearly out a my chest.

"Kate and Essie Lou, Momma2's here with Sheriff Joe Taylor and his deputy man. She keeps tellin' that sheriff you be our cousins, so I'm guessin' you best be sayin' that, too, on account of him and his deputy havin' guns. He don't seem like his visit with y'all is gonna be friendly."

I was scared to my bones for Kate and Essie Lou. Kate went straight to Essie Lou and put her arm 'round her shoulder. Essie Lou was cryin' and held the baby real tight to her like someone was gonna take it away. I heard steps comin' down the trail and knew it would be Momma2 with the sheriff. I could hear Momma2 talkin'.

"You see what y'all gotta see and then you make a beeline back to Siloam Springs, Sheriff. Cousin Kate and Essie Lou gonna be livin' with me on this place fer as long as they want to. Essie Lou done had her a baby boy, yesterday, and she's feelin' pretty weak today. You don't need to be makin' her feel any more pain than that mean husband she run away from. I don't care what Doc Gibbs and y'all think those two girls is doin' here, but they doin' nothin' but mindin' they own business tryin' to get away from the bad man Essie Lou married. They come down here to be safe with me, and those two crackers hurt 'em worse than that dumb husband of hers. They don't need no more hurt comin' to 'em. They'll answer y'alls questions, then you be off my land. You understand what I tell y'all now."

The sheriff must a stopped walkin' 'cuz I could hear their feet stop. "Miss Lila, law's the law. Those Putter twins done told us some tales on those two girls you callin' cousins. Ain't right and ain't normal fer two women livin' together unnatural like them two boys told me. They tell me they saw 'em lovin' on each other the ways of a man and woman. Law says unnatural livin' gives me reason to send 'em to jail or the crazy house and take that baby away. You sayin' they y'all's cousins don't make it so. You got proof, Miss Lila?"

Momma2 spoke slow and steady. "Proof, Sheriff Joe—you wantin' proof on my word? I give you proof." Momma2 said the next part real slow and deep. "I said Kate and Essie Lou are my cousins and that's your proof. Poe and me lived here since 'fore y'all were born. Your daddy and Poe was friends, Sheriff Taylor. You forgettin' that? Poe carried your pappy to his grave. You forgettin' who you's 'supoose to believe? I never had to prove my word to nobody, and I don't plan to start now. You takin' the word of them cracker twins down the road and you put a question mark on mine? You go ask Kate and Essie Lou if'n they my cousins, and they gonna be sayin' what I said. Don't y'all go askin' me fer proof a my word again. My word's my proof!"

I never in my seven years ever heard Momma2 tell a lie, and I never heard her tell it so I would believe her. My mind was swimmin' from her lyin' and the new thoughts it put in my head.

I could hear the sheriff's feet start to walk, and pretty soon, I heard a knock on the door. Kate walked over real slow and opened up the screen door.

"Ma'am, my name's Sheriff Joe Taylor. I gotta clear up some business 'bout the two a you girls. I heard some tale on y'all, and I come ta find out how y'all be livin' here. How y'all know Miss Lila?"

Then I heard Kate make a story out a the words I just come ta tell her. She told the sheriff Essie Lou and her moved to Siloam Springs to stay with their cousin Lila. She told him Essie Lou's husband beat on her, so Essie Lou run to Kate and Kate drove 'em both to Lila's house where they couldn't be found. She told the sheriff Essie Lou's voice didn't work on a'count a the hurt her husband give her. I listened to all of them stories comin' out and thought their story would make a library book someday, it was so real like.

"Them Putter boys done told me they seen you two women do unnatural things, and I need to put that to rest. What y'all think they seen? You two dykes? We don't want no queers in Benton County."

"Kate dropped her eyes. She took a breath; then there was a mighty long pause 'fore she answered the sheriff. "I'm not sure what they saw, Sheriff. Essie Lou and me are real close cousins, and she hasn't been feelin' real good with her being pregnant. I suppose they could make up any kind of story to fit their minds. We love each other, that's for sure. But we love Lila, Tilly, and Junie Bird, too. That doesn't make us unnatural does it?" She looked at him straight in his eyes as she told that story.

The words "dyke" and "queer" was new words to me. Didn't fit no sentence I heard 'fore, and they didn't seem like words Kate liked either. 'Sides that, "Unnatural lovin'" didn't seem like two words that belonged together. Lovin' was lovin'. There was nothing unnatural 'bout that!

I saw the sheriff lift his head like he was thinkin' on somethin'. He looked at Kate and then looked over to Momma2. He spoke slow and low and the sound comin' out a him was growlin'. "I know I ain't got no proof 'sides the story a them Putter boys, so I s'posin' I don't got no call to take y'all in. But I'll be tellin' y'all this. Siloam Springs ain't no place fer any queers livin' here. I see or hear different than what y'all tellin' me, I be back to see y'all. People ain't gonna be lookin' at ya like y'alls cousins. Y'all hear what I'm sayin'! I ain't forgettin' Poe, Lila, but this ain't 'bout Poe. It's 'bout the law and I'm doin' what the law tells me I ought to do. You hearin' me, Lila?"

All of us heard him 'cept Zeke, and I knew I'd tell him the story fer the day was over. He'd never believe all the lyin' that went on.

Momma2 spoke 'fore Kate could. "Oh, we hear you, Sheriff. We heard ya loud and clear. Now you hear me. You, your deputy, and nobody else who's got bad business with us is welcome to come to my land. You did your duty and you come and met my cousins. You listened to some dumb boys sneakin' up on my land with no good on their minds and you believe 'em. You believe 'em 'cuz they make a story 'bout two people never done 'em one bit a hurt. Their story brings my family trouble, and we didn't ask fer it and we don't want it! Now, get off a my land and don't be comin' back!" Momma2's voice was ever' bit as growly as the sheriff's when she did her talkin'.

"We be goin', but if'n we need to come back, we'll be back. Don't be thinkin' you be the law, Lila. I'm the law here." He finished with that threat then turned to head up the trail. I heard him and his deputy stop at Kate's car and talk, but I couldn't hear no words they was sayin'. Momma2 put her arm on my shoulder and opened the screen door to the slave house.

Kate was standin' by Essie Lou who was holdin' her baby, and I could see Essie Lou shakin'. Her scared hands was holdin' the baby like maybe she'd drop it if'n she didn't hold it tight as she was. Kate petted her head as Essie Lou leaned into her.

"You two girls are safe with me. Y'all hear me? There's no reason fer y'all leavin' here unless you're wantin' to leave. There's a fancy red car not doin' much up by my house and don't suspect it needs to go anywhere with you and that new little baby. We may not be cousins, but we's a family just the same. This here's your home."

Momma2 went over to the chair Essie Lou was sittin' in and put her hand on her shoulder. She patted her shoulder, then bent over and peaked in at the baby. "You got yourself a beautiful son, Essie Lou. Only thing y'all got to be thinkin on is makin' him grow up strong and happy. Y'all are safe here."

Essie Lou looked over to me. Her voice was soft and weak. "Tilly, Momma2 is a brave woman. You wanta be just like her when ya grow up." She had tears fallin' down her face the whole time she was talkin'. Momma2 shook her head at what Essie Lou said.

Kate was watchin', then she spoke, "Essie Lou is right, Tilly. Your Momma2 is brave. Doing the right thing, when everyone else thinks it's wrong, is brave and she is brave."

Then Kate turned to Momma2. "Miss Lila, I should be better in a week or so and will help Zeke in the orchard again, if that works for you."

"That will work just fine, girls. I'll look forward to y'all comin' up to the house fer dinner tonight, if'n y'all feel like it. I'm thinkin' Junie Bird would like to see that new baby boy of yours. It'll be nice havin' y'all back at the table." Momma2 started fer the door then she stopped and looked at Kate and Essie Lou. "Oh, and girls, this morning 'fore I tried to talk sense into that sheriff, I stopped at the court house. It's important to register that new little baby in the town records, so he gets a proper birth certificate. I put Harris down for his last name. I figure cousins need the same last name, don't you? With that, Momma2 left us all standin' there thinkin' on what she said.

Chapter 18

It took weeks 'fore I could stop thinkin' the sheriff was comin' down the road ever' time I heard a noise, but, pretty soon I stopped worryin' on it. The apples was bein' picked, and we was busy with all our regular business. The barn was full a apples, and the smell was coverin' the air with its sweet. I knew we'd be makin' apple cider 'fore long, and Momma2 would have bruised apples to make my favorite red jam.

Junie Bird had finished her big quilt and it was layin' on Momma2's bed. It was beautiful with its reds, oranges, purples, and yellows. It looked like an artist done painted it with cloth. Junie Bird was on to makin' a new quilt, and Essie Lou and her new baby boy was right there helpin' her. Essie Lou had the baby tied 'round her belly with a big ol' tea towel. Seemed she didn't want that baby to ever get off a her belly. He just hung in that ol' towel and stayed there 'til she had to feed him, then she took care a that business and back he went, curled up right by her heart.

Junie Bird took to that baby like it was a needle and thread. She cooed and hummed over it like a bird in a nest. Ever' time Essie Lou would bring the baby to the house, Junie Bird would put her hands together and make a squealin' noise that near drove me crazy. Essie Lou was a good momma to her little baby boy and to Junie Bird, too. She took to carin' for both of 'em.

Kate was workin' in the orchard with Zeke again, but he let her do most a the tractor ridin' on account a her havin' to walk slow with her bottom still hurtin'. Her brusies was gone, and, 'cept fer her scar over her right eye and her walk, she was Kate again. Her hair seemed curlier in the moist heat of the apple season and it fell on her face like a lace doily. Her cheeks, red as apples, smiled again, and it made me happy inside to see her dimples pokin' in her face.

Momma2 was busy with ever'thing the harvest brought to the orchard. She had pickers workin' all over the orchard gettin' apples off a the trees. They looked like ants on a hill the way they climbed in the branches and on the ladders to get to the apples. The boxes in the barn was fillin' up fer cash money.

Wasn't much to make Zeke show his happy, but he showed it a lot when Kate said she was comin' back to the orchard to work. That fancy red car was still sittin' by the side a our house, not goin' anywhere.

Ever' Saturday, when Momma2 and Zeke went to get supplies, I done stayed at the house to watch the family as Momma2 started callin' ever'body. I was a pretty good watcher she told me.

Kate and Essie Lou didn't have no reason to be goin' off to town. Kate was workin' to get better, and Essie Lou was busy bein' a momma. I heard Kate call her "Little Momma" and that seemed to stick with how we all was gonna call her now that she had a baby boy. Kate and Essie Lou still didn't call that baby anythin' but "sweet baby." It was a funny name to tag on to a person, but it wasn't my business, so I called him that, too. Seemed like we all got back to our life pretendin' no sad had happened.

On one warm September mornin', Momma2 told me she was gonna be needin' my help in the garden to get all the vegetables in the house fer cannin' and into the root cellar fer storin'. After I done all my mornin' chores, I went out to the garden and started pickin all the vegetables that was ready to be picked and puttin' 'em in the baskets Momma2 done told me to put 'em in. We was both busy with our work. Momma2 was bent over a row a pole beans, and I was on the other side a her. We was both pickin' 'em clean. "Tilly," Momma2 said. "You gonna be turnin' 8 years old the end of this month. Time we talk about you goin' to the school in Siloam Springs."

I stopped my bean pickin' and looked over to Momma2. "Whatcha y'all talkin' 'bout, Momma? I'm learnin' right here where I live! I don't need no school to be teachin' me. I don't think you got a good idea at all."

I was talkin' with a deep sound I heard Momma2 use when she meant something real important.

"Well, Tilly, you are a mighty smart girl, I know that." Momma2 didn't stop with her bean pickin'. "Smart doesn't go away, that's for sure, but it can get better and school is gonna make your smart better. Next week, I'm takin' ya in to school to register ya to go."

I couldn't pick beans and listen to Momma2 talk 'bout me leavin' the farm to go to Siloam Springs to school with people I didn't know and stay in a buildin' all day without fresh air. I was feelin' sick.

"Tilly, I know how good y'all are readin', and you know your numbers good as anything. Don't expect y'all have any problems with the other book learnin' they be givin' ya. Not ever'body's smart as you—best you do something with it. The bus will be pickin' ya up and takin' y'all to school after harvest."

"Momma2, I can't be goin' to no school way from the orchard. I got to do my chores and help y'all with the family. I don't want to go to school!"

My voice choked on the last words makin' Momma2 look up from her pole bean pickin'. "Tilly, your Grandpa Poe and me both went to school. If your Grandpa Poe would still be livin' he'd a sent ya to school soon as they would a taken ya. I let you grow a bit and run wild 'fore I'm makin' ya go, but I am makin' ya go, now. You get to learn, Tilly, and that's a mighty good thing to get ta do. Y'all will go on the bus when the time comes," she said, real firm like.

Momma2 started bean pickin' again, and I let the water in my eyes run down my face while I worked with the beans. I couldn't 'magine leavin' the orchard and my family to go to some damn school with stupid damn people. My mind wanted to say ever' bad word it held in it, and my voice wanted to say 'em out loud. I decided I wasn't gonna be talkin' to Momma2 again 'til she changed her damn mind.

I continued to help Momma2 in the garden, and I did ever'thing she told me to do, but I didn't say no words to her. When we finished and I left the garden, I still wasn't talkin'. I spent that night and the whole next day without any words comin' out a my mouth, just like Essie Lou when she first come to our place. When I went to bed the next night, I covered my head with my Junie Bird quilt and let my tears soak the blankets. Pretty soon I heard my door open and felt a body sit on my bed.

I heard Momma2's voice, "Tilly, there's nothin' in the world I wouldn't do fer ya, girl. You're my heart and soul. I never expected to have ya to love, but I got ya, and I am thankful for ever' day I do."

The quilt was still over my head, but I was hearin' Momma2's words come through it. My ears was hearin', but my heart was not wantin' any soft words to try to sneak in on it.

"Life is not always easy. It gives ya choices, and it's what ya do with those choices that makes a difference for good or not. I'm the only one to help ya make good choices, and I need to do it. I want ya to learn, Tilly, and use your good head to do good things when you get to make your own choices. School is not a bad thing. It's good. I'll miss havin' ya here with me, but I want this fer you 'cuz it's a good choice."

Momma2 gently pulled the quilt down off a my head. "Tilly, some people don't get a choice on how their lives get worked. You may not know it now, but y'all are lucky to have a good brain and people who love you. It's the best start anybody can have, and I want ya to make the choice to be happy with goin' to school when it's time. I love you, Tilly, and it's that love that makes me make the hard choice fer ya."

I could hear the choke in Momma2's voice, and when I looked at her straight on, her face was streaked with water from tears. I pushed the quilt off'n my chest and reached up with both a my arms and put 'em 'round her neck. I hugged her with a tightness I never hugged. She hugged me right back, and we was both cryin'. When it felt like we was finished with our bawlin', Momma2 put her hands on the top of my head and pushed my hair back a my face. She smiled at me, then kissed me on top a my head. I lay back down on my pillow. She put the quilt tight to my neck then left the room. I still didn't say no words, and she didn't say any more either, but when I woke up the next mornin' and come out a my room, I said "Good mornin'" to Junie Bird and to Momma2 'fore I even sat down to breakfast.

The next Monday, Momma2 drove me to the school to get registered. It was a big ol' brick buildin' with a lot a windas that had frames on 'em. They looked like the squares of Junie Bird's quilts, I told Momma2. She just grinned down on me.

We walked up the stairs to a door and went inside. There was a door to our left held a woman busy with papers. The lady wore glasses that had pointy ends on 'em, and she looked like she was real important. Momma2 introduced herself, then pointed over to me. This here's Mathilda Mae Harris. She'll be goin' to your school this year after apple harvest. Momma2 nodded over to a bench by the wall, so I walked over to sit and wait fer her.

Momma2 filled out the papers she needed to fill out as I sat real quiet waitin'. When she was finished, she took the papers up to the important lady and gave 'em to her. "Matilda Mae Harris goes by the name a "Tilly." She reads anything y'all give her, and she can do any number figurin' ya put in front a her. She'll be eight years old when she starts comin' to this school, but you put her with a teacher who knows how smart Tilly is. Tilly will be one of y'all's best students."

Momma2 braggin' on me made me feel ten feet tall. I got up from the bench when she said good-bye to the important lady and put my hand in Momma2's as we left the buildin'. When we got to the truck, Momma2 said, "I think this calls for an ice cream cone, Tilly. It's not ever' day someone in our family gets registered fer school."

Momma2 and me got in the truck. As Momma2 put the key in the starter place, I saw the sheriff's truck pull up. The sheriff got out a his ol' truck, and I started to wring my hands free of the water they was makin'. After that day the sheriff and his deputy come to our house, Grandpa Poe's gun was hangin' behind our heads in the truck, and I was hopin' like hell Momma2 wasn't fixin' to take it down and use it on Sheriff Joe Taylor.

Momma2 didn't look to the sheriff"s truck. As he started toward our truck, Momma2 put the truck in reverse and started to pull out a the place we was parked. She was goin' real slow, and I could see the sheriff real close to her side a the truck. I heard him say, "Lila, stop your goddamn truck." Then he put his hand on the side a Momma2's truck door and hit it with his hand, so's she knew he meant business. Momma2 stopped her truck. The winda was already rolled down on account a it being so hot, and we needed the air when we drove.

"What ya doin' stoppin' me?" Momma2 growled. "You always in the habit a botherin' people mindin their own business?" I could tell Momma2's red haired temper was fixin' to flare up.

Sheriff Joe Taylor was at the winda of the truck. He was a tall man and even taller with his sweaty ol' hat on. He was eye level to Momma2, and now they could see one another eye to eye. His voice come through the winda. I stared straight ahead worried he'd see the scare in me.

"I been thinkin' a lot 'bout those two cousins you got livin' with y'all." He hung on to the word "cousin" and drug it through mud 'fore he was finished sayin' it.

"Them cousins still down to your livin' quarters? I 'spect the law might need me to be checkin' in on 'em from time to time to make sure they livin' up to the law. You know the law, Lila. I gotta do what the law says I gotta do."

Sheriff Joe Taylor was usin' the word law to sound like he was doin' somethin' good when I could tell he wasn't. I knew that sure as Momma2 did. She was starin' straight ahead when he was talkin'. When he finished, she turned to look at him.

"No laws being broken on my orchard, Joe. We mindin' our own business and growin' apples. That's all we been doin'. We're hard workin' people, you know that. Best you find law breakers somewhere else and don't be botherin' us none."

Momma2 talked real nice, but I could see her hands on the wheel of the truck, and saw her knuckles were white from holdin' it so hard.

"Well, I been thinkin' on that, Lila, and I got myself a little idea. Seems you don't want no law botherin' you and them cousins of yours, and well." Sheriff Joe Taylor put his hand on his hat and rubbed on it like his head was thinkin' real hard. He paused then continued, "I'm needin' me a new car. You can see that ol' truck over there 'bout to be off to the salvage yard." Sheriff Joe Taylor was talkin' like a radio man, all steady and low like he was wantin' Momma2 to believe what he was sayin'. She turned to look at him dead in his eyes.

"I figure it this way. If'n I got myself a brand new red car, I wouldn't have no time to be drivin' out to bother you and them cousins of yours, and well, we'd be doin' each other a big favor with that idea of mine. That's a pretty damn good idea if'n if I say so myself." Sheriff Joe Taylor kinda chuckled. Then he took his arm off Momma2's truck winda and stepped away.

"I ain't forgot Poe and y'all's goodness, and this here idea of mine settles y'all's good with mine. You think on my idea, Lila, and I'll be out next Saturday afternoon to see them cousins or pick up my new car. I'll have my deputy drive me out 'case he needs to help me enforce the law. Ya see I got me a written statement from two eye witnesses sayin' they seen them cousins of yours doin' things the law says is not natural. Laws the law, and that piece a paper gonna be mighty strong in a court a law. 'Course, if'n I got me a new car, I sure will find a way to misplace that piece of paper, and that deputy of mine will drive my ol' truck back to Siloam Springs, and I'll drive off in that pretty, red car. We'll be done with any business we have with each other. Guess y'all be decidin' which one I'll be doin'."

Sheriff Joe Taylor took a breath after all that talkin' then tipped his hat to Momma2 like he was some fancy man and turned to leave. Momma2 spoke up and her voice carried over to him.

"Don't y'all **ever**!" She said "ever" like she used every letter in that word. "And I mean **ever** use Poe's name again. You don't deserve to have that man's name come out of your mouth. You hear me on that, Joe Taylor?" Momma2 opened the door of the truck and stepped out. She walked over to Sheriff Joe Taylor and spoke up to him with muscle in each word. "I reckon you got yourself a new car, beings as we don't have any other law 'cept yours, and you sure aren't law. You ain't any better than them white sheet crackers scarin' people and makin' life miserable 'round here. Your pappy would be ashamed of you 'cuz I know I'm not so proud to know you myself. Things be what they be. You come out and get your car Saturday, and you bring that piece of paper with you. That be your cash money for that car. You hear me on that?"

That was all she said. She turned 'round and got back in the truck. She put the truck in reverse and drove us straight to the ice cream shop with no other words. We walked in ta that shop bold as could be and ordered up ice cream cones. I picked strawberry on a'count a the color and Momma2 picked chocolate. We took our ice cream cones outside and got in the truck to head home. On our way home, Momma2 turned to look at me. She was lickin' her cone and smilin' one of her full mouth smiles. I couldn't, for the life of me, think why she was doin' that when the sheriff just put her in a fit. "Tilly, we best be gettin' back to our family 'fore they think we got lost somewhere in Siloam Springs."

Momma2 gave me a wink, then turned her head to look out the windaw. She headed us home. Both of us lickin' on our ice cream cones as she drove. My mind was stirrin' something fierce, what with gettin' registered for school, and hearin' Sheriff Joe Taylor want Kate's car. I was wonderin' what Kate would have to say 'bout that?

Chapter 19

Durin' apple harvest ever' day was pickin' day, and the orchard workers was busy pickin'. They was almost done with it, and the trees that looked all red and green last month was mostly green now, and the red on 'em was sittin' in the barn gettin' ready for the big trucks to come and pick 'em up to take to the train station.

When the trucks come to take the apple crates to the station, Zeke and the darkies workin' for him put a big ol' hoist by the boxes. They'd wheel that hoist to pick 'em boxes up and then steered 'em to the truck to be loaded. That was a job caused 'em all to sweat. That day would be comin' soon.

I heard Momma2 and Zeke talkin' last night after supper 'bout their Saturday trip to town and their talk with Mr. Callaway down to the freight shop 'bout settin' up a time to pick up the apples. Zeke told Momma2 he thought the apples would be ready to go by the followin' Monday. That meant it would be the week 'fore I turned eight. Then I'd have to start school in Siloam Springs on account of apple harvest bein' over. I wasn't wantin' that day to come, even if'n it meant we would be makin' apple cider and havin' us some of Momma2's birthday potato salad and apple pie.

I was runnin' 'round the orchard on this Friday not payin' any attention to what the workers was doin'. I was runnin' past the barn when I saw Momma2 down talkin' to Grandpa Poe. That was her quiet time, and I knew better than to go runnin' in on her talkin'. I watched her from the fence place.

She had her head bowed down and her chin was restin' on her hands. I saw her run her hands through her thick red hair while she was talkin'. I couldn't hear what she was sayin', but I knew it was somethin' important, on account a her turnin' her head this way and that while she was talkin'. Kinda like she was arguin' with herself.

When I was a little bitty girl, Momma2 walked me down to Grandpa Poe's place and sat me on her lap. That's the first time I heard her talkin' to his stone. She introduced me to him like he was right there standin'. I 'member it just like it happened yesterday.

I reckon' Momma2 was tellin' Grandpa Poe all 'bout that Sheriff Joe Taylor and how he was makin' Kate give him her car, so's he wouldn't bother us none. I know that didn't set right with Momma2, but if Kate gave the car to the sheriff, then Kate and Essie Lou and their "sweet baby" wouldn't be leavin' here, and I was likin' that part of it.

When we drove back from Siloam Springs, after registerin' me for school and meetin' with Sheriff Joe Taylor, Momma2 told me to go inside the house and see to Junie Bird. She said she wanted to go to the orchard to talk with Zeke, then she wanted to talk with the girls down to the slave house. She was gone a long time.

While she was gone, I took my library book to the porch and sat in the wicker chair with the big pillow. I curled up in it and read my new book on butterflies. It had all kinda pictures and told about each one. Some of 'em butterflies was from countries I never heard of. I s'posed I'd learn where those places were when I go to that damn school.

When I heard the back door open, I went back inside the house and saw Momma2 gettin' pans out to cook our supper. I knew she was gonna fry up some taters and side meat 'cuz she had a bag of taters from the cellar in one hand and a slab of side meat from the smoke house under her arm. She started peelin' the taters and sliced 'em all up in cold water. She let 'em sit there while she fried up the side meat. She put the side meat on the table, then she put those taters in the side meat grease to get 'em all brown and crispy. Momma2 made the best taters ever.

I had put my library book by the radio table and asked Momma2 if'n she wanted me to set the table for supper. She looked over to me and smiled. "Tilly, that would be mighty helpful."

I set the table for our family which was now six of us. We all fit on the benches Grandpa Poe had built real good. Momma2, Junie Bird, and Essie Lou and her baby, tied up to her belly, set on one side. Me, Zeke, and Kate sat on the other. I put down six plates, six forks, and six knives 'cuz the side meat would need cuttin'. When the taters was almost done, Momma2 told me to go outside and ring the bell to tell Zeke and the girls it was eatin' time. The bell hung on the side of the house by the back door. I hit it with the stick hangin' by the bell. I hit it three times good and loud.

I stood outside for a minute just lookin' 'round. I saw Kate, Essie Lou, and their 'sweet baby' come up the trail first. I could hear 'em whisperin' while they was walkin'. Kate was walkin' a little bit better now. A whole lot better than when she first got that broom pulled out a her bottom. It made me sad just thinkin' on that again. Essie Lou had her sweet baby tied 'round her waist with that ol' towel, and she just looked like Essie Lou all pregnant with the baby on the outside of her belly instead of the inside.

They both waved when they saw me standin' there. As soon as they got to the trail place that met up with the trail over to the barn, they waved over to Zeke. I hadn't heard him comin', but when I looked over, there he was. His overalls was clean and ready for supper. The sun was settin' low in the sky, but it hit his head just right, and I could see silver threads runnin' through it. I thought he looked like he was mighty important with that silver on top of his head.

Kate and Essie Lou waited 'til Zeke got to where they was. When he got there, Essie Lou pulled the towel away from the baby so's Zeke could see him. That sweet baby was getting' big, and I was thinkin' Essie Lou was too little to be carryin' him around like she was. She was a little momma that was for sure.

Zeke bent over to look at the baby; I could see him smile big as Sager Creek. He put his finger out like he was gonna be playin' with that sweet baby. He talked to him real soft and gentle and made little noises that seemed to fit a baby's ears. The baby woke up and looked at Zeke. I was wonderin' on if he knew Zeke was gonna be his friend 'cuz who would know it, but that there baby smiled a real smile.

He was gonna on seven weeks old, and his little face had changed so's it didn't look so wrinkled and red. Essie Lou combed his hair down and made him look like a little baby man. He was kinda cute, if'n I say so. I think Zeke thought he was just right 'cuz that's what he kept on sayin'. "You's is just right, little man, you's just right."

I knew Momma2 had talked to Zeke, Kate, and Essie Lou about that damn ol' Sheriff Joe Taylor, but none of 'em was talkin' 'bout it. They was just lookin' and talkin' over that baby. Essie Lou tucked that baby back inside her towel place, and we all walked into the house together.

Junie Bird was already at the table in the middle of the bench on the door side of the kitchen. Momma2 sat next to her, so she could get out of the bench if'n she needed to get somethin'. Essie Lou sat on the other side opposite a Kate.

Momma2 passed the side meat to Zeke first, then he passed it to me. Zeke didn't do no prayin' at our table on a'count a Momma2 wasn't the prayin' kind. She passed the taters to Junie Bird, then when the plate got to the end of the line, Kate and Essie Lou traded side meat and taters. Both plates ended up at Momma2's and she put 'em in the middle of the table 'case someone wanted another helpin' of one of 'em. I was hopin' there'd be taters left for me to have a second plate.

We didn't say much at the table that night. Momma2 was quiet and so was ever'body else. I guess sometimes thoughts make too much noise in your brain to let your mouth talk. That was how it was for me. My brain was thinkin' on how that Sheriff Joe Taylor would come and take that beautiful car from Kate. Then I thought maybe she wouldn't let him take it, and he'd take her away from us and maybe take that sweet baby. My mind was goin' all over the place with my thoughts. One of my thoughts was that Kate and Essie Lou and that sweet baby would just go drivin' off in their fancy red car and leave that damn ol' Sheriff Joe Taylor without a red car. All those thoughts made me feel sick in my stomach and pretty soon those taters wasn't tastin' as good as they use to. I was gettin' ready to put my fork down and stop my eatin' when I hear Momma2 start to talk, "Poe built this here table for a big family, and now it has it. I'm mighty glad about that."

I looked up to Momma2's eyes, but they was down on her plate. Kate and Essie Lou looked down, too. Sweet baby started makin' noises in that towel place a his and Essie Lou peeked in to see what was goin' on. She looked up then. "Miss Lila, I'm thinkin' this sweet baby a mine is mighty glad this here table fits us all, too. He a smilin'."

Kate looked over to Momma2. "Miss Lila, if you don't mind, I'll ask Tilly to help me clean up that red car of mine on Saturday morning for its new owners. I don't want him to think he's not getting the best car in the world."

Momma2 nodded over to Kate, then turned to me. "Tilly, you heard Kate. She'll be needin' your help Saturday mornin' after you get your chores done. You do what she needs you to do to make that car shine. You hear me?"

"Of course, I hear ya, Momma2, you're sittin' right here aren't ya?" I wasn't bein' sassy with her, I just wanted her to know there wasn't anythin' wrong with my ears.

"I'll help Kate with anything she needs. I'll shine that car up real good."

Kate actually smiled when I said all that, and it made ever'one at the table seem like a light went back on. 'Course ol' Junie Bird didn't figure in on any of this 'cuz she was eatin' and that was all she was thinkin' on.

Zeke excused hisself from the table and went and put his plate in the sink. He thanked Momma2 for the good food then walked back to the lean-to for a night a sleep.

Kate and Essie Lou got up from the table when we was all done and cleaned up the dishes. They had taken that chore from me when they first moved here and they was still doin' it. I helped by pickin' up the plates and puttin' the taters and side meat in the ice box.

Junie Bird went and sat by the radio 'cuz that's what she did after she ate supper. Sometimes Momma2 turned it on and sometimes she just let Junie Bird sit there and be quiet. Like I told ya, Momma2 was big on quiet time.

When the dishes was all done, Kate and Essie Lou told Momma2 they was gonna be goin' down to their house. Kate said, "Miss Lila, I'll be getting up early tomorrow morning to help Zeke get ready for the last day of picking. We should be getting some sleep. This little baby doesn't seem to know when it's day or night, so we try to grab sleep whenever we get a chance."

She smiled over to Essie Lou when she said that, and Momma2 nodded her head like a yes was comin'. "Get a good night's sleep, girls. If'n you need somethin', you just come up and get me. I'm here for ya."

We all went to bed early that night that Sheriff Joe Taylor told Momma2 he was needin' a new car, and Momma2 had had to tell Kate and Essie Lou that story. Seemed like the day had had too many hours in it.

Now it was Friday and tomorrow I'd help Kate polish up the red car for Sheriff Joe Taylor. I was thinkin' on that, and I figure'd Momma2 was fillin' Grandpa Poe in on the same thing. I just kept quiet at the fence place watchin' her talkin' to him. She was there a good long time 'fore she picked herself off the bench and turned to leave. I wasn't payin' attention at that minute, so she saw me by the fence. "Tilly, I just told your Grandpa Poe you're goin' to be goin' to school after your birthday. He's real happy about that, and you know you can't never have too much happy, don't ya?"

I thought about that for a minute. I liked that happy feelin' I got inside a myself, and I knew what happy felt like. Goin' to school didn't seem to me like it was goin' to make me get in that happy place. Momma2 wasn't tellin' Grandpa Poe what was right on that subject.

Chapter 20

I was eight years old when I woke up this mornin'. I didn't feel any different, but sure e'nuf, it was true. I put on my overalls with the yellow patches Essie Lou done fixed up for me, when I tore 'em climbin' out of the tree, then opened my bedroom door. There, right in the middle of the floor, was the prettiest packages I ever did see. They was wrapped up in regular brown paper, but there was material tied in bows all over 'em. Next to the packages was sittin' Momma2, Junie Bird, Kate, and Essie Lou. The sweet baby was layin' on Essie Lou's lap lookin' up at her makin' baby noises. Zeke was sittin' in the kitchen on one of the benches watchin' me. Kate started to sing a song all about happy birthdays. I never heard that song 'fore, but she knew it all the way through. Junie Bird got in her happy place when she heard Kate sing and started hummin' to the noise inside her head. Momma2 put her hand on Junie Bird's hand; that made her hummin' quiet. Momma2 had a way with Junie Bird; she had just the right touch. I could see the smiles all over the room.

I had sleep inside a my eyes and I wiped it away, but water was with it. I didn't know I had tears, but there they was and they was happy ones.

The tears I had last Saturday was not happy ones. They was from a sad place I couldn't get away from. When I woke up last Saturday, I knew I was gonna be helpin' Kate with her car. I ate my breakfast and did my chores, then went down to the slave house to tell Kate I was ready to help her. When I got there and looked inside a the house, Kate was by the table with her head in her arms, and I could tell she was cryin'. I knocked real soft. She looked up at me and wiped her eyes with the back of her arm. Essie Lou was givin' her sweet baby some of his breakfast, and she was cryin' too. When I saw both of 'em cryin', I couldn't stop the tears comin' out of my eyes. They was sad tears.

I never really had anything of my own like that red car, 'cept my arrow heads by my bed, but I was thinkin' it would be real hard to give somethin' away that was your very own and especially somethin' you didn't want to give. I s'pected that was why they was cryin'. I was cryin' on account a I didn't like to see Kate and Essie Lou cry. It made me sad in that place where my heart felt like it hurt.

Kate come to the screen door and let me in. She put her arm 'round my shoulder and tugged me to her. "Don't be worrying on us crying, Tilly. We're just remembering buying that old car and driving in it. Let's you and me go get it shined up for its new owner."

Kate went over to Essie Lou and gave her a kiss on the head. Now that I knew they wasn't sisters, I knew the kiss was a Grandpa Poe kiss, and it meant she was loved. She touched the sweet baby's head, then went to grab us some rags from a box they had near their sink. She got a big bucket from the porch, then we went up the trail to go clean the car. When we got near to the Eve tree, I slowed my steps to see if'n Kate was gonna be scared to go by it. She didn't put no mind to it. She just kept up her steps to mine, and we went on by it.

When we got up to the car, Kate looked over to me. "You know, Tilly, you never had a chance to ride in this little beauty of a car, did you?"

I shook my head "no."

"Let's you and me take it for a last spin down the road before we clean her up. What do you think?"

That was like askin' me if'n I wanted cotton candy. I put my hands in the air and squealed like a little pig. "Miss Kate, I'd like that just fine."

Kate opened the door to the car and I jumped right in. She got in on the other side and put the key in the starter place. She turned a little knob that made the top of the car roll down on it's own. She got back out of the car to put some straps on the top, so it wouldn't fly away. She got back in and started drivin'. The wind wasn't even blowin', but my hair was swept away from my face when the car started down the road. I could feel that air blowin' 'round me, and it felt so good I wanted to stay in that car forever. As we drove down past the orchard, Kate put her hand on the horn that let Momma2 and Zeke know we was on our way.

We drove down the straight part of the road headin' to Siloam Springs, and when we got to the turn sign to town, Kate stopped and turned the car 'round and headed us to home. I put my hands in the air on the way back— that made me feel like a bird in the sky with air all 'round me. When we got back to the house, Kate turned the car off and put her head on the wheel. I was quiet. There was no wind and the only noise in the air was the sounds comin' from the orchard.

"Miss Kate," I said with my words real soft. "Are you okay?" I asked, hopin' she was. Her face come up from the wheel, and she looked over to me. "Yes, Miss Matilda Mae Harris, I'm fine. How about you and me get this car all shined up for the taking?"

With that we got out of the car, filled the bucket with water, and started washin' that beautiful red car down with our rags. We washed it twice—once to get all the dirt off of it from sittin' so long and from the road ride and the second time to get it ready for shinin'. The shinin' part was the hardest 'cuz it took rubbin' and that rubbin' work made me sweat. Kate was sweatin' too.

When we was all finished, it was as shiny as a red jewel. Kate went over to the car and opened the door. She looked inside of it, then turned 'round and spoke to me. "Tilly, no thing on this earth is more important than the people you love. This car is just a thing. It's a pretty thing, but it's just a thing."

I nodded my head to her with a "yes" nod. She smiled back to me.

Kate threw the water from the bucket on some flowers Momma2 had growin', and then she come over to me and took my hand. "Let's go get Essie Lou and that little boy and go down to Sager Creek for a good swim. I don't think that Sheriff Joe Taylor needs to ever see us again."

We run all the way down the trail whoopin' and hollerin' like we was both seven years old. We passed by that Eve tree like it was as safe as ever, and when we got to the slave house, we opened the door to find Essie Lou sweepin' the floor. The sweet baby was in the apple crate that was his bed. I could hear him makin' baby noises like he was talkin' to himself. "Essie Lou", Kate said with a lift in her voice, "let's bundle that sweet little baby up and all go down to Sager Creek for a last swim. It's gonna be getting too chilly to do it much longer and it's a perfect day to get wet." After we got Essie Lou and the baby ready to go, we went up to the house and made Junie Bird ready to go with us. Momma2 was out in the barn with the darkies gettin' the apples ready for pick up. I run to the barn to let her know what we was doin'. She told me to be careful and have fun.

It seemed like a whole new thing havin' people to go play with in the orchard. It's like my wish for a sister come true, only it wasn't 'xactly like I wished. I got me two big sisters and a little brother, only they wasn't my blood.

We played in the creek for a long time. While Essie Lou played in the water, I sat on the bank of the creek and watched the sweet baby sleep. Essie Lou had fixed a little place where the sun couldn't get to him, and he was happy as could be sleepin' outside. I thought maybe some night when he got bigger, he could sleep on the shed top with me under the stars. We could have us a real good time, I was thinkin'.

When we got all tired out, we went back up to the slave house where I left Kate and Essie Lou, and I went home with Junie Bird. As she and I walked up to the house, I reached over and took her hand. She grinned a big grin, and I held on to her hand tight as I could. Junie Bird was my mother. She carried me in her belly and on the day I was born, she had to hurt to get me into this world. I thought of that while we was walkin', and it gave me a tight feelin' in my chest for her. She could drive me plumb crazy when she chased me 'round or hummed her crazy hum, but she was my real momma and I could feel that in my heart.

When we got to the house, I could see the shiny car sittin' in the spot we parked it. I was hopin' that damn sheriff woulda already come to get it and we'd be done with his business. That is not how it happened. It was near to dark when we heard a truck comin' down the road with it's lights on. It squealed to a stop in front of the house. It was Sheriff Joe Taylor and that dumb ass deputy he hauled around with him ever' where he went.

We'd already ate our supper and we was sittin' on the porch. Kate and Essie Lou had stayed at the slave house and hadn't even come up to the house for supper. They wasn't wantin' to see that cracker ass sheriff.

When we heard the truck, Momma2 had the rifle ready by her side. She had taken it out of the truck this mornin' 'fore I got out a bed and put it on the porch. She told me to keep my hands off of it which I sure 'nuf did. Now she had it by her side as she walked outside. Sheriff Joe Taylor and his deputy was out a their truck and was walkin' over to the red car. I heard that Sheriff Joe Taylor whistle a long low whistle when he come on to it. He turned to see Momma2.

"Ain't nothin' like a new car to make a man feel like a million dollars, is there, Miss Lila? I see the keys are in the ignition. It looks like it's shined up and ready for the takin'. I don't suppose I need to see those girl friends of yours to get the paper work changed over to my name, do I?"

Momma2 walked over to Sheriff Joe Taylor. She still had Grandpa Poe's gun in her hand. " The titles in the junky box, with the signatures on it. You take care of makin' it yours at the county house. Don't you even think about goin' down to see Kate and Essie Lou. You aren't welcome here any more, Joe. You get in the car and you drive away. Don't you ever come to my property again. I'm sorry I ever knew you."

With that Momma2 lifted the rifle to her arms and stood there waitin' for Sheriff Joe Taylor to get in Kate's car and drive away. His deputy was standin' there with his mouth hung open like he was waitin' for a fly to land on his tongue. He looked dumber than them stupid ass Putter twins. I watched 'em all from behind Momma2. Junie Bird was in the house, Zeke was at the barn, and Kate and Essie Lou was down at the slave house with their baby boy. No one talked for a minute. Sheriff Joe Taylor started walkin' toward Momma2, then she pulled the gun from her arms and put it in the crook of her arm like it was an umbrella.

"Lila, I'll be headin' down the road in my new car. I want ya to know you ain't foolin' me with them two queers you got livin' in the slave house. You can call 'em your cousins, but I ain't as dumb as you think I am. Ways to find out stuff, bein' a sheriff, and I know them two is dykes. I got ever' right to haul both of 'em out of this land and take 'em to jail or put 'em in the crazy house in Little Rock. I'm takin' the car and leavin' you be. That there's my thank you to Poe. We're even."

With that, Sheriff Joe Taylor turned his back to Momma2 and got into Kate's shiny red car. That stupid ass deputy of his got into Sheriff Joe Taylor's truck. They started up the vehicles they was in and started down the road.

When they was out of sight, Momma2 walked over to the house and walked in. She went to her bedroom, and when she come out, she didn't have Grandpa Poe's gun. I figured she put it under her bed where it belonged. That's where it needed to stay.

She walked down to the slave house, and I followed her. We both went inside. Kate and Essie Lou was waitin' for her to say somethin'.

"Girls, we got us a truck that we use to drive to town to get what this family needs for food and supplies. We been usin' it for years and seems like it works just fine for all of us. We'll be goin' to town next Saturday, and you'll be welcome to come along if you be feelin' like gettin' out of this here orchard for a while. You let me know when you feelin' like you want to go."

Momma2 turned to me. "Best we get to bed, Tilly. You gonna be turnin' the clock on eight years old next week, and I'm not gettin' any younger." She put her hand out and I took it. We walked up to the house and went to bed. The red car was gone.

Chapter 21

I wasn't thinkin' on anything, now, but my birthday. Momma2 looked at me, "Tilly, we all got you a little something for your big eight year old birthday. Ever' one of us. We all want you to know we're happy you are turnin' eight and goin' off to school.

I walked toward ever'body in the room who was sittin' 'round those packages. I went first to Momma2 to say my good mornin' with a big hug to her. Then I went to Junie Bird, Kate, Essie Lou, and finally I walked over to Zeke. He had a big grin on his face as I walked to the kitchen bench. "Good mornin', Zeke." I put my arms around his waist as he sat there. He hugged me so tight, I could feel his breathin' as I hugged. When I finished with my Zeke hug, I heard Momma2 say, "Tilly, it's Saturday and we got to be goin' to town before the sun sets. Get on over here and open y'all's presents.

There was a part of me that was so excited I could hardly get my legs to move toward those pretty packages, but the other part of me was kinda shy about it all. I never, in my eight years, had a family like this makin' my birthday any more than potato salad, birthday apple pie, and a happy birthday wish. Today made my day feel like I had my own private Christmas. I felt like I could be the baby Jesus himself with all this celebratin'. I walked over to the packages and Momma2 handed me the biggest one. She told me it was from Junie Bird.

I took the package and sat down on the floor with it in front of me. I untied the material ribbons 'round it and it opened all on its own. I could see right off it was a brand new quilt. It was beautiful! It was made with all different colors of red—my favorite color in the whole wide world. When Junie Bird saw it open, she clapped her hands in the air and flapped her arms like she was goin' to go flyin' off. "Birthday, Tilly, Birthday, Tilly, Birthday, Tilly". She said it three times like I was a deaf person.

She was still clappin' her hands when I got up off the floor and walked over to her. I put my arms 'round her neck and hugged her tight. "Thank you, Momma," I said, like it was true. She was my momma even if'n she couldn't be a real one to me. Junie Bird stopped clappin' her hands and put her arms 'round me. She hugged me back for the first time in my life and laid her head on top of mine. When she was finished with her huggin', she put her hands in the air. "Birthday, Tilly, Birthday, Tilly." Momma2 had to tell her to stop talkin' or she might of kept on sayin' it 'til I turned nine.

The next package was the second biggest package. I could tell that's how Momma2 was gonna be givin' 'em to me. Biggest to littlest. I figured that out right away. She said, "That there package is from Essie Lou." I looked up at Essie Lou and she was smilin', not just with her mouth, but also with her big, brown eyes. She was lookin' like that picture show girl again. "Go ahead, Tilly." Essie Lou said, "Open it up." I could see how excited she was for me to get goin'.

I opened it up, and inside that package looked like a rainbow. One on top of another was dresses. I counted 'em. There was seven. One for ever' color of the rainbow. I couldn't believe my eyes. They was dresses with sleeves that was puffy, and there was a dress that had straps for shoulder places. They all had ruffles and fullness I knew I could twirl 'round and make a full circle of material.

"We all know y'all is gonna be the smartest girl in school, but I wanted y'all to be the prettiest one, too. Them dresses gonna do that trick." Essie Lou said with a grin that spread 'cross her face and made it look like a light was in it.

I got up from the floor again and walked over to Essie Lou. I put my arms 'round the place that didn't have sweet baby and gave her a hug. "Thank you, Essie Lou. They are the most beautiful dresses my eyes ever did see. Them Malcolm girls ain't seen nothin' like 'em."

I don't know why that made ever'body laugh, but even Zeke was laughin' at my words. Momma2 handed me the next package. It was a square box. When I opened it, my eyes looked at Momma2. "Yes, Tilly, that's from me," she said. "Try 'em on."

They was a pair of brand new shoes. They was brown shoes with black tie stings. They was as shiny as a new penny. "They are called Oxford shoes," Momma2 said like I should know what they were, but I didn't. I just knew they was new shoes and they was mine to wear with my new dresses. I was beginnin' to think school might just be a good choice for me.

I went to Momma2 and put my arms 'round her and hugged her tight. "Happy Birthday, Tilly." She said soft like she was singin' it to me. She reached over to the smallest package. "This here's from Zeke. He made it for you."

I opened up the package and inside was the most beautiful wooden box I ever saw. It was copper colored wood, and it was polished to shine. On the top of it was carved my name. On each side of my name was a little apple with a leaf on each apple. It looked like it come from Mr. Tribble's store, but Momma2 had told me Zeke made it for me. I sat there with it in my hands and just starred at it. It felt like it held a secret treasure. "It's a school box, Tilly. Zeke made it from the apple wood we got growin' on the orchard. Now you don't have to leave the orchard 'cuz you got a little bit of it with you when you go to school. Go on, open it up."

My hands lifted the lid of the beautiful wooden box. Inside, it had three wooden pencils all sharpened and ready to write and an eraser for any mistakes my pencil might make. It also held a box of eight crayons that were brand new. I looked over to Zeke. His eyes was wet with tear water. I got up from the floor and ran to him. I put my arms 'round him tight as I could. I hugged him with all the love I felt for him and let my tears run down my face without shame. "Thank you, Zeke, for my box. It's real beautiful." I pulled back from him so he could see my tears was comin from my heart, too. He tussled my hair. "You's welcome, Miss Tilly. You's my girl, too."

When I turned to look at the room of birthday, I saw ever'body cryin' 'ceptin' Junie Bird. She wouldn't know why to cry. Her happy place made her hum, and when I was as happy as I felt right now, it made me cry. Maybe Junie Bird's way was better.

Momma2 looked over to Kate. Kate looked at me. "Tilly, you gotta go outside for my present. I couldn't wrap it up."

Zeke went out the back door. When we all got outside, Kate told me to head on down to the slave house. She said ever' body would follow the birthday girl. I started to skip on down.

Fall colors was all 'round us; it looked like someone come in over night and painted up the bushes and the trees. When I was comin' on to the Eve tree, I stopped dead in my tracks. I saw the ropes first. They was four of 'em. They was hangin' down from the branch that use to hold my swing. There at the bottom of two of the ropes was a new swing seat. It was painted red. A ways away from my swing was two longer ropes that almost went to the ground, but at the bottom of it was an apple crate. I turned to look at Kate. She and Essie Lou was smilin' and lookin' at me. Junie Bird was hummin' in her head, and Zeke and Momma2 was starin' down at the apple crate. I could see Momma2 look at Zeke, then Momma2 turned to Kate and Essie Lou. I looked over to the crate, then I looked at all of 'em. There on the crate in bright red letters was these words, each on a different line of the crate. It read:

Ezekiel

Poe

Harris

I could see there was a bright red pillow inside the crate ready to fit that sweet baby.

"Miss Lila and Zeke, we'd like our sweet baby to carry this family's names when he gets old e'nuf. Kate and I's hopin' you'd find that to be okay with y'all." She made that last sentence sound like a question.

Zeke and Momma2 both stood there for what seemed like forever 'fore Momma2 spoke her words, "My Poe would be honored to have his name carried on. I'm mighty happy to know there'll be a new little Poe livin' on this orchard. And I'm thinkin' Zeke is gonna feel the same way 'bout his name gettin' to be carried on. Ezekiel is a strong name and your sweet baby is gonna grow up to be a strong man, just like Poe and Zeke." She turned to look at Zeke. "Am I right how you thinkin', Zeke?"

Zeke looked at Momma2 and then to Kate and Essie Lou. "I's gonna take care of you two girls and your sweet baby 'til ol' Zeke goes in the ground by my Belva and my baby girl. That little boy be called my name and Poe's name makes ol' Zeke's heart feel like it could jump out of my clothes. I'm 'special thankful to y'all for chosin' my name for your sweet baby. "Special thankful." Zeke said that last part twice, makin' sure they knew he was glad their sweet baby was named for him and my Grandpa Poe.

Essie Lou walked over and handed the baby to Zeke. "Seems this little boy would like to have his first swing. Would y'all mind pushin' him a bit?"

Zeke picked up sweet baby and walked him over to the apple crate. As gentle as a leaf fallin' from a tree, he layed that baby inside the crate on the soft down pillow. He pushed the swing gentle as could be and that baby made soft noises as he moved through the air.

I heard Kate's voice talk over to me. "Go on, Tilly," she said. "Try yours out. Looks like its gonna fit you perfect."

I still stood there. I looked at Kate, then I run to her and put my arms around her waist. "Thank you, Kate. I don't rightly know how to thank you."

"Well now, you can thank me by getting on that swing and seeing how high you can get it to go. Seems to me that tree's been missing you playing on it."

I took my hands from 'round her waist and run for the tree. I jumped up on the bright red seat and started pumpin' my legs to get it goin'. Pretty soon I was in the fall colors of the leaves, feelin' the air blow past my face and push my hair back like when I was sittin' in that shiny red car. There was no shiny red car, but there was Kate, Essie Lou, and their sweet baby. They was all better than any car could ever' be.

Zeke was pushin' that sweet baby, and Momma2 was holdin' Junie Bird's hand to keep it from flappin' in the air. Kate had her arm 'round Essie Lou while they watched us swing in the Eve tree.

It was gonna be Sunday tomorrow, and we'd be makin' apple cider a'count of apple season bein' over, and we had apples ready for it. On Monday, I'd put on one of my rainbow dresses and my new shoes and carry my school box on the bus to Siloam Springs to start school.

Today, Momma2 and Zeke would go to town to get supplies and while she was gone, Essie Lou would bake my birthday apple pie. I was guessin' Momma2 already had my potato salad made for our dinner.

I looked down from my swing seat and saw my family watchin' me swing in the Eve tree. They was all in their happy place and so was I.

Epilogue

Today, even though progress has been made, the LGBT community still continues their fight for their civil rights.

US vs. Windsor, 570 US 744 (2013) is a landmark civil rights case which held that restricting the interpretation of "marriage" and "spouse" to apply only to opposite-sex couples is unconstitutional by the Defense of Marriage Act (DOMA).

The Obergefell case of 2015 made same-sex marriage the law of the land. Every state has to recognize those marriages now, but legal fights to put both mothers on birth certificates, along with other issues continue to be legal battles for these couples.

Cheryl Kathleen Maples, an Arkansas pioneer and attorney began her legal fight for same sex marriage in early 2013, after a discussion with her lesbian daughter regarding the Windsor case. She spent six months researching and creating the marriage lawsuit. She began her challenge to the state's laws on July 1, 2013. Hers is the first post-Windsor lawsuit in the country. She fought tirelessly for equal marriage rights for the LGBT community until her death. She had a little Momma2 in her. Countless others, continue to fight for justice for all.

Kate and Essie Lou are fictional characters that represent the real love and commitment between two people. In Tilly's words, "what's unnatural about lovin?"

About the Author

Born in Colorado in 1947, JS Fairchild grew up in Gunnison, CO, a college town near Crested Butte. She attended her local college and received her MA in education. She is married, has two daughters, and three grandchildren. She has lived, taught school, and worked in education for 40 years in Delta County, Colorado. Now retired, she writes, hikes, plays pickleball, volunteers at the Grand Mesa Arts and Events Center, and enjoys her family and friends.

Made in the USA
Middletown, DE
07 January 2023

20891869R00106